GNOME WAY HOME

A Long Way Home Novel

RAYMOND S FLEX

A FLAWED PARADISE

FLAUGHTERBERT LET GO of the handles of his cobbled-together wooden wheelbarrow, chocked high with chewed-up rocks—rocks he'd personally mined on out of the shaft—and he wiped his brow clean of the steady film of sweat that'd sprung up there with the back of the sleeve of his tunic.

A hard day's work almost done, just another day down till the day he would die.

He looked out ahead of him, over the bluish glade which marked out this hill, the biggest hill in the whole of the Dwinns, his home Domain, and he peered out of his short-sighted eyes— eyes that'd only got worse from all these years in the gloomy underground chewing up rocks—to the lop-eared bunnies hopping about and the birds doing that twittering they always seemed to do.

He dug into the breast pocket of his tunic, one which had once upon a time been quite fine, and had been bespoke threaded down at Gnoming Threads in the village of Earknork, his home village, but had, over the years, been relegated to the status of work clothing and as such was now all frayed and torn all about the place.

Which was to say nothing for how his tunic now near enough failed to cover the ever-expanding belly which seemed to jut out from him a little more with each passing year.

His tunic was weaved with a fetching blue and green plaid design, though you wouldn't have known that without being told, since it was so caked in mud that no colours had a chance of shining on out . . . even in the glorious, beaming sunlight that *always, day after day* shone down on the Dwinns.

From the velvety insides of the breast pocket of his tunic, he fished out a toothpick, which was a fairly euphemistic way of describing what others might have called a stone pick, or something similar. And certainly, the way that he had to go about the stone pick, digging right in between those gaps in his teeth, would've snapped a toothpick in two if it dared so much as think about it.

Good thing toothpicks don't tend to do an awful lot of thinking.

He got his mouth shot of all that stone dust, bending down and giving his mouth a good wash with the mountain spring which sprinkled out from the rock face like a naturally occurring garden tap.

But with *much* colder water.

Though the water was pretty much tasteless, it tasted a darn sight better than having a mouthful of stone dust.

As he straightened himself up, feeling the warmth of the sun beaming down on him, Bert let loose a long and not particularly contented sigh.

How did he *get* here?

To this point in his life?

Sometimes living in the Dwinns got him down. Oh, it wasn't like it wasn't *pleasant*, because it was, actually, in truth, it was totally and completely pleasant, and there really wasn't anything wanting about the place.

Not one thing.

Still, all the same, Flaughterbert, or simply *Bert*, as he was known to his friends, longed for something different, to go outside the frontiers of his safely mapped-out Domain, the place he had grown up and where he would surely die at a satisfyingly old age.

But, before he did all that, before he dedicated himself to his garden and looked for a fetching lady gnome to settle down with, he was determined that he would see something of Gnomelandia, go out there and see something of the world.

Everyone was always telling him just how dangerous it was— how there were lots of very nasty gnomes just lurking in shadowy places, all ripe to rob him of all his gnomic valuables. But, somehow, Bert had always thought that was so much bunkum.

Gnomes were the biggest thieves there were, that much was true, but to his mind at least those 'bad' gnomes out there were honest about their ways.

Because the residents of the Dwinns certainly weren't.

He really hadn't ever invested too much thought into this whole fear of the 'outside' world.

He knew that really, deep down, the gnomes who said those sorts of things were just *scared*. And Bert knew that he couldn't for the life of him live scared, not even for so much as a single moment.

Why, just walking down the cobbled streets of Earknork on a quiet Sunday morning, he could scare even the most rigidly built, square-shouldered gnome with a well-timed "Boo!"

No, it was clear that everyone in the whole spread of the Dwinns knew that there was a certain *badness* out there, just ready to bring its, very clawy and extremely frightening, paw down to bear on everything that the gnomes who lived here knew and loved.

So why didn't they do anything about it?

Why didn't anyone ask the difficult questions?

Why was the matter never raised in town meetings—why were the topics always restricted to who would be on street-sweeping duties that week, or that perennial question of who would water the flowers in the hanging baskets?

No one ever talked *defence*, nothing like that.

And, for one, Bert was sick of it.

Why, if any such *bad* force wanted to take hold of the Dwinns, it'd only have to breathe its horrible, and no doubt halitosis-ridden, breath over the gnomes living here and they'd send half the population to an early grave from a heart attack.

Well, Bert *was* going to ask those questions. He was sick and tired of how things got swept under the rug here, and how the big issues never *ever* got truly solved.

He would be the one to ruffle the feathers, that was right, that was it!

With an extremely final, and brute-strength tug on a particularly nagging pebble stuck between his lower teeth, he pocketed his stone pick back into his breast pocket, snatched up the handles of his wheelbarrow, and overturned his load onto the pile of chewed-up rocks.

One more load.

Just one more.

And it was quitting time.

ROCKING THE BOAT

BERT GOT HIMSELF all washed down in the mountain pool at the exit to the cave he'd dug out so lovingly, and, it seemed, so long ago.

One thing was for certain, independent mining around here was an absolute *boon*. No other way to describe it. And anyone who didn't go in for it, any of the others who wasted their time on fishing or, *worse*, gardening, needed their heads looked at in his opinion.

In his one hundred and forty years working that same old mine, cranking out the silver and the gold, and the occasional diamond, he had become an *extremely* wealthy gnome.

Though respect, so far, had eluded him.

He felt the chilly water wash over his gnome skin, carrying away all the rock dust that'd clung to him through the day. And he drank the water too. Enjoying the coolness inside his mouth, seeming to function as a kind of elixir after what had been another hard day's work.

From his trouser pocket, he withdrew a bar of fudge he kept there to chew on while he paced his way down the mountainside. He took a bite of it. Got that lovely sugary goodness flowing about his mouth, and then he began his journey down to his criminally *huge* mountaintop mansion . . . though, in truth, there was nothing criminal in the way he'd amassed his fortune.

It had been quite easy really.

First, he'd had to be mean, and second, and really built into the first, he'd had to say *no*, a lot.

He really had become the expert at saying no.

He'd said no to orphanages, to those programs they did for elderly gnomes that'd lost the ability to control their bladders, he'd said no to the ones who'd wanted to collect up some cash to re-thatch cottage roofs, and the like.

. . . And he'd sat back, rather smugly actually thinking about it, and watched on as each and every one of those programmes that'd come to him asking for money had been stung, one by one, by claims of corruption, or mismanagement, or *incomplete* taxes, etcetera, etcetera, etcetera.

Gnomes who made their money by pretending to be running charitable organisations were thick and many throughout the Dwinns, that was for certain.

And Bert had seen them all off with his innate meanness.

All those scammers. It sickened him to think of it.

If there was one fault that he would've single out gnome-wide, all throughout the Dwinns, if not the entirety of Gnomelandia, it was that there was really no entrepreneurial spirit at all.

Hardly a scrap of it among them.

Even the scams they thought through were half baked.

Why, a case in point was the tax system.

Of course, whenever tax time rolled around, Bert paid everything he owed, sometimes more. And he would always—*always*, without fail—send off his return with a personal, *hand*written note to the Chairman of the Dwindian Council, imploring him to invest in a rudimentary defence budget.

Just get some gnomes on board with some spears, and some bows and arrows, that sort of thing. He knew that it would've been in vain to go right after asking for a nuclear submarine, or a high-flying bomber . . . no it was best to start out small.

Bows and arrows and spears.

That would be a start.

They could *build* on that, year upon year.

And every year Bert got a reply from the Council, one of those infuriatingly *form* replies which thanked him very nicely for his concern, thanked him for paying his taxes ahead of time, and wished him all the best in the New Year, while gently reminding him of next year's due date for his return.

No, it was no good, no good at all.

And to think that Bert had sucked it up for years and years, stacked up those notes from the Council, allowed them to get away with inaction.

With *criminal* inaction, for so long.

Nope, he was his own boss, and so he could afford to give himself a day off.

He *was* fabulously wealthy, after all.

So wealthy that other gnomes just didn't know what to say to him.

He guessed that they wanted him to tell them his secret, but he often reasoned with himself that that would've been like trying to teach a fish how to walk on coals.

Even if the fish had a great desire to be a hot-coal walker, there was that simple and devastating mismatch of biology, physics and—probably also—chemistry there.

A simple improbability, brimming on the impossible in all honesty.

Nope, Bert declared that today, a Tuesday, he was well and truly fed up of gnomes and had decided that now was the time for him to make a difference.

To *really* go on the warpath and sort out this place, once and for all.

A CRIMINALLY HUGE, MOUNTAINTOP MANSION

OFTEN BERT would overhear gnomes walking past his criminally huge, mountaintop mansion jabbering about among themselves, talking about how it was ridiculous that the whole mansion was made out of marble, and buffed to that incredible shine.

But Bert knew they were just jealous.

Jealous that they built *nothing*.

That the only asset they'd managed to cobble together in their one hundred years *plus* of life was a half-arsed capacity to trick other gnomes out of their own money.

On those long summer evenings, draped over his moleskin sofa, Bert would often think over just how things managed to keep on ticking throughout the Dwinns, how the whole infrastructure didn't just one day totally collapse.

In the end, he settled on a few factors.

The first, and probably the biggest thing behind the success of the Dwinns, was that, really, there wasn't all that much infrastructure to grind to a halt.

Oh, sure, there were the cobbled streets that needed sweeping from time to time, and the flower boxes that needed watering, but there was no cohesive form of public transport. Only the odd horse-drawn cart here and there, and that was only the more enterprising gnomes.

Refuse?

Bury it in the garden.

Running water?

Dig a well . . . or just take your bucket off to the nearest stream (that was the most preferred method among the gnomes of the Dwinns).

Yes, it was fair to say that, all things considered, there wasn't all that much throughout the Dwinns that was held together by sweat-inducing hard work.

But then there was the other thing, the fact that most gnomes throughout the Dwinns just got by tricking one another into giving their money away.

The charity trick, of course, was the old favourite, and no matter how many times gnomes went banging on doors asking for donations for an extremely vague-sounding old folks' home, or an orphanage racked with suspicion, gnomes, on the whole, gave generously.

Bert surmised that the only way this worked was that there was an innate understanding amongst all gnomes that they had to keep up the pretence of all these proposals being genuine. Because, if they raised a complaint, the next time that they themselves went about with their own fraudulent scheme there would be a shortage of goodwill towards *them*.

Furthermore, Bert supposed that the simple way that the Dwinns functioned was by their being a finite amount of money bobbing about the place, and it, simply, being moved about from one gnome to another.

Bert tried to put those things out of his mind for the time being. At the front door of his mansion, he shucked his working clothes, and put on his fluffy, pink dressing gown: the one that he'd been given by some long-forgotten aunt—or had it been an *odd* uncle?—and which he greatly enjoyed putting on over his otherwise-naked gnome body.

He breathed in the air of the place. That cool draught that smelled of nothing else but the slick marble which the whole mansion was made up of. He also caught a light odour of lavender, and recalled that his cleaning lady, Tilda, had come by today.

She was one of the few gnomes he'd come into contact throughout his life that had actually taken on some degree of honesty and responsibility, and had done well to carve herself a little niche in the working landscape of the Dwinns.

Armed only with her feather duster, and her polishing rags.

Though one day he had found that one of his silver spoons had gone missing, he had made nothing of it with Tilda—didn't think so much as to raise it as an issue with her.

She was doing her best to fight against her well-engrained gnome nature.

And, anyway, it wasn't like he had any proof of what she'd actually done.

All he had was circumstantial evidence and a pretty thorough understanding of how gnomes acted when no one was watching.

But, no matter, it wasn't like he was hurting for money . . . like, at all.

Bert chomped on the last bites of his fudge, swallowed it down, feeling his mouth tingling with the sugar spread out all over his tongue, and then he slumped onto his moleskin sofa, lay there for a few moments clearing his mind of the day he'd just had, of his day down the mine.

He stretched himself out, feeling all his muscles unknotting, and his heart slowing down to a gentle *pitter-patter*.

It was so *pleasant* here, what off up in his mountaintop mansion, on the hillside *he* owned.

It was like he could just stay here forever.

He could almost breathe in the silence that enveloped him.

Could hear the breeze blowing through the tufts of grass on the hillside all about his mansion.

And he knew, tomorrow, everything would be different.

Tomorrow the revolution began.

COME THE REVOLUTION

T HE NEXT DAY turned out to be a bit of a dog.

Bert woke in his bedroom to that dampness in the air, and he couldn't help but screw up his eyes with a little sense of awe at the day all spread out before him. He could hear the wind howling through the nooks and crannies of his mansion, could hear it rattling the windowpanes. The *patter* of raindrops pasting themselves against the glass.

As he threw off his duvet, and threw his dressing gown about his naked gnome body, he had second thoughts about venturing out to see the Council in gnome today.

In putting today—a *Wednesday*—down as the first day of the New Times . . . as he'd christened them the night before while lying on his side and waiting for sleep.

He almost didn't dare peel back his pale-yellow, velvet curtains, but he finally found the strength to do it. And the day outside didn't look much better than it sounded.

The rain lashed down in sheets, only punctuated by the occasional *clap* of thunder and the flash of lightning.

It was on days like these that he truly wished he wasn't a gnome—that he didn't have a naturally built-in alarm clock, a body clock so atuned that it could wake him up at the same time every day . . . or, well, within about five minutes' accuracy.

Because he would've loved nothing better than to get himself back into bed and to pull his frumpy duvet over his head, and write this one off till tomorrow.

But, even though he'd been a self-employed business owner for a solid one hundred and forty years, he had yet to take a day off from mining, and as he was going to *have* to take several days off to go see the Council, he knew that he couldn't simply waste it slouching about in bed.

So, it was with more than a couple of yawns that he went about cobbling together his expedition kit . . . which was to say, a *makeshift* expedition kit since he'd never once been on an expedition in his life.

The expedition kit, in the end, turned out to include: a pair of wellington boots, a knapsack with wooden toggles, two jumpers—it got frosty going through mountain passes—three tunics, six pairs of woolly socks, six pairs of woolly underwear, a spare pair of trousers that looked appropriate for trekking (they'd at least served him well on those colder mornings as he'd venture on up to the mine).

The kit was rounded out with a trusty, though beaten-up, brass compass.

Bert had been a little surprised to dig the thing out from his wardrobe, but he had some sort of a vague memory of a long-forgotten uncle—or had it been an *adventurous* aunt?—leaving this compass to him in some will.

Bert's memory wasn't what it had once been when he'd been a spritely eighty, or ninety, year old.

Come to think of it, it'd most likely been a *great* uncle or aunt.

Bert had got himself to the doorway of his bedroom when he realised that something was missing. That he'd just about gone and forgotten that old travelling adage . . . and no wonder since he'd never had any need to actually implement it, it was only something he'd heard from those quite odd, *extremely* beardy, travelling gnomes.

When it comes to travelling take four times the cash you think you need.

And so Bert burrowed on deep into his underpants drawer, and got himself a fresh few wads of notes, enough for him to pay for a fairly comprehensive renovation of his mansion.

Hopefully outside the Dwinns wouldn't be as uncompromising as everyone said it was.

He could *really do* without someone mugging him for the cash, though he estimated he could quite easily make it up with a solid month's work down the mine.

Bert got all his kit downstairs, and packed away in his kitchen, and then he set about making himself a hearty breakfast of bacon, scrambled eggs, brown toast—with hefty amounts of butter all spread over it—which he then followed up with a mighty mug of coffee which really set him off ticking.

Next, with full belly, and alert mind, he swept about his cupboards, lashing together a couple of ham and cheese sandwiches that'd help him along his journey.

The way he saw it, these would just be emergency measures since he fully intended to dine out en route.

What was the point of him having established such a successful independent mining operation if he couldn't so much as save time eating out as he went on?

No point, that was what.

Before long, he had everything all together. He had his expedition kit all ready for him to go. He jammed on a pair of sturdy walking boots, ones that he often used for mining. They would see him through fine.

Only as he latched open the front door of his mansion, and looked on out at the lashing rain outside, did he have second thoughts and switch out the walking boots for his wellies.

Much better idea.

After he'd thrown his anorak about his shoulders, he also stuffed his lucky red stocking cap over his thick thatch of blond hair, and jammed it on down over his angular ears.

That'd see him right.

As he stood there, on the threshold of his house, looking on out into the dingy grey skies which were bearing down on his hillside, and his house, he felt a stiff breeze blow up against his cheeks, felt the blood rush up to his head, and his heart give a little skip.

Yes, this really was something that he'd never have imagined doing himself.

But here he was, doing it.

And that, really, was the end of it.

No turning back now.

Not once he'd set his mind to this thing.

Without so much as a glance back over his shoulder, he

brought his front door shut with a *slam*, and he ventured on out into the cold, dismal day, and towards the Dwindian Council.

DARKNESS LURKS IN THE LIGHTEST PLACES

G ENERAL ARDULL knew his charges often referred to him as simply 'Dull' behind his back. He knew that they all said that because he wrote poetry. He had heard the rumours, just like the rest, but he couldn't care less.

It was one thing to be a poet and a general, and another just to be a standard, fleabag recruit.

His life had depth, theirs had none.

His heart carried fire, whereas theirs only carried blood.

. . . Thinking about it, that wasn't too bad . . . if only he had had his notebook handy.

Ardull clutched his hands behind his back, at the base of his spine, and he writhed them.

Writhing his hands was a bit of a habit of his, just something he couldn't help doing whenever he felt annoyed or, often, when he was simply thinking.

He recalled one of his underlings once telling him that

writhing his hands made him look somewhat maniacal, and that had stung, just a little.

But he'd cast it off because he knew the *real* truth about himself.

He was a businessman, like any other.

And that was where his concerns exclusively lay.

Let them think whatever they wanted to about him . . . just as long as they didn't stand in his way he wasn't all that bothered about how he got his results.

And so he spread his broad shoulders, and gave his greasy, black, side-combed hair a flick-through with his fingers then gazed on out through the leaf-green tent flap and out to the bright sky that beamed on down over the desert hills that rolled on away from their temporary headquarters.

They'd been marching for about six hours when Ardull had given the order for them to down their packs and to set up tents.

It had been a bit of a long haul, and everyone was deserving of a break.

He could feel the sun warming up the tent about him, and he caught that familiar, if a little *sharp*, scent of sweat oozing off the fabric. This tent had belonged to Ardull's predecessor and, if he'd had to make a guess, he would've said that he hadn't quite prioritised personal hygiene above all else.

That, or he'd been a skunk.

Ardull chewed on the yaltas leaves, making them all gooey with his saliva, and slushing them into the side of his cheek with his tongue. They were fairly tasteless, which was to say that they tasted of leaves, and not much else, but what he liked about them was the way they seemed to send his pulse racing, and the blood driving up to his head.

While they'd pushed on through the Thrushbury Forests he'd had his gnomes grab hold of them by the bagful, and he'd counted a solid dozen or so horse-drawn carts worth of them.

Unfortunately, they had no horses.

Or carts, for that matter.

They'd lost them all in the last jungle, to various bogs, and quicksands, and sunning crocodiles.

But the yaltas leaves would come in useful later, Ardull was sure, they'd help out with the monotonous marching that they'd been doing a lot of lately, and which he anticipated them doing a good amount more of before they crossed on out of this, the Poot Domain: a strange hodgepodge of jungle and desert, and into the much more consistent, mild, and *leafy*, Domain known as the Dwinns.

The Dwinns was just ripe for the taking.

And Ardull intended to take the place.

He'd done his research, back in their home Domain of Juttle. They'd got word from the scouts that the Dwinns didn't have so much as the very basics of defence.

Not even a basic conscription system.

It was like the place had been designed for a Juttilian takeover.

If Ardull and his gnomes didn't take it over, it would only mean another band of gnomes would beat them to it. And as his father, an army gnome just like himself, had often said if a gnome didn't take what was there for him then he would only find what he had being taken from him.

Outside his tent, Ardull could hear the gentle *chatter* of his men, all of them chomping down on their evening ration of soup.

That was good, they'd need their strength for the coming march.

Though it was true that the Dwinns had nothing by way of organised defence that wasn't to say that the gnomes would give themselves up without a fight.

He anticipated them all rising up against the invaders, trying to keep hold of the place that they called home.

Just as Ardull would've fought with all the strength he had to keep hold of Juttle.

And, in a way, that was what he was doing now.

It was just a pre-emptive strike.

Because, one thing was for certain, the Dwinns surely wouldn't remain a sitting duck forever. Some day, *someone* would have the bright idea of investing in defence, and a full-out war would be an entirely different matter.

Ardull's merry little band: no more than a thousand gnomes strong now, was only suited to what his superiors termed 'Arrive and Occupy.'

And that was what they had set out to do in the Dwinns.

A week, maybe a few days more, and then they'd be there.

They'd seize hold of a whole other Domain.

THE PATH TO GLORY IS A SLIPPERY ONE

T HE GROUND just seemed to be flowing out from beneath Bert's feet.

Every time he brought the rubber tread of his welly down, his foot just seemed to get away from him, and he had to grab hold of a convenient jutting-out rock, or a tuft of grass, to steady himself.

The constant rain wasn't exactly helping either.

He could hear it drumming on down at the hood of his anorak. His skin was damp with perspiration since his anorak seemed to have lost whatever 'breathability' it'd once held as a garment. That unpleasant smell of his own sweat seemed to press against his nostrils and mouth, making him feel kind of claustrophobic despite being out in the open.

He chomped on a block of fudge, at least trying to keep himself warm on the inside, while outside he turned, slowly, into a block of ice.

He steadied himself up against a rock and glanced out from beneath the hood of his anorak.

It was no good.

He could only see about ten, maybe fifteen, paces about him.

The curtain of rain just covered all else.

Though he could only see a little way, he saw enough about him so that he could make out the sheer slope of the hill to his left-hand side, and he knew that the drop would be real enough if he slipped on the muddy path.

Despite having lived up a hill most of his life, despite *living* in a mountaintop mansion, he had never really had a head for heights.

That, he supposed, was the definition of irony.

He clung on tighter to the rock on his right-hand side, and glared out into the rain, trying to divine whether or not it was getting lighter.

Whether or not the sun was threatening to make an appearance here at any point.

His conclusion was inconclusive.

He dug out his compass from the pocket of his anorak, gazed over the twitching half-white, half red, needle, and he saw that he was still heading in the desired direction: due east.

He estimated that he'd been going for about three or four hours now . . . as a gnome, he didn't have much use for a watch, or any sort of time-telling device.

He just followed his nose, so to speak.

But, that said, the weather, or any sort of turmoil seemed to play havoc with a gnome's time sense, just like it did now.

He had hoped to be in a nearby village called Phardoe by

now, and he really hadn't much idea whether or not he'd just gone on past it.

He'd never actually visited Phardoe, and so it would be entirely understandable if he *had* . . . but he had always had such a clear idea of where it was, and a clear idea of how to get there, that he'd never had the heart to convince himself of anything else.

Bert blinked back the rain which now soaked his face—tried to blink it out of his eyes. There was little point in him trying to wipe the water away with either his hands or the sleeve of his anorak, because both were just as soaked as his face.

So he just sucked it up like the hardened gnome he was.

As Bert glanced up from the compass, out to the dreary path stretching out ahead of him, he thought he caught sight of a form out there.

For a second he couldn't contain a slight sense of disbelief, that there was someone just as mad as him, someone who'd actually stride out in weather like this.

. . . And he'd just about stumbled into the conclusion that he was *glad* to see another soul up here, and in such *dreadful* conditions, when he realised just what the shape was. Not another gnome.

A dog.

A TRAVELLING COMPANION?

"WHY, HELLO THERE, DOGGY," Bert said.

Bert listened to the throaty growls. He knew the sound of rabies when he heard it.

A ragged, curly-haired animal with great big gnashing teeth. Its fur was clotted with mud, and it had powerful flanks that suggested it hunted for necessity.

The dog rushed at him, from out of the gloom, mouth foaming and eyes a decidedly *evil* red.

Right as the dog bundled up to him, ready to take a bite out of his calf, Bert aimed a short, sharp kick at the rabid animal's belly and sent it tumbling off down the slope with a vaguely fatal *whine* as it went.

SO NOT A TRAVELLING COMPANION THEN?

Nope.

LIGHT ON THE HORIZON

ALL THINGS CONSIDERED, Bert never once thought of heading back along the trail, of going on back to his criminally huge mountaintop mansion. He was determined to put one foot in front of the other and just to keep on heading on towards his destination.

He put the rabid dog out of his mind, and began to wonder if it was just him or if the rain really was letting off, just a little bit.

Yes, as he brought the hood of his anorak down to feel the raindrops on his face, he felt the downpour reduced to only a fine mist.

A fine mist that was still *awfully* wet.

But a fine mist all the same.

Visibility had improved, too, and he found that he could not only see his own hand in front of his face, but he could see a little further along the path also, down into the lush green valley which dropped away to his left-hand side.

No longer did he feel that unearthly need to stay so close to the rock face on his right so that he grazed the material of his anorak.

Funny how visibility could do that.

As he trekked on for another solid half hour, he soon made out the colour breaking through the mist. The red roof tiles up ahead.

Phardoe.

At last.

He consulted his innate sense of gnome time and found that it was approaching midday now, he would arrive to the village just in time to have a spot of lunch, and not before time either. He could feel his stomach giving unpleasant little rumbles, no doubt already caught off guard by the last of the stone dust being swallowed down into it.

As he munched harder on his sugary lump of fudge, he felt his muscles growing tighter, his heart beating faster in anticipation, and he knew that he could hardly wait to see the village up ahead.

He had spent a lot of time back at his mansion picturing Phardoe, wondering just what it would be like.

Funny that it was only now that it had occurred to him to actually visit there.

And, to tell the truth, it was only really a stopover.

The path sloped downwards, and into the fine blanket of rain that continued to fall.

The sun was threatening to break through the cloud cover and he could already feel it warming him just a little.

As he pounded onwards, he found himself egging the sun on,

encouraging it to break on through the cloud and dry him out before he got down to the village.

It did as he wished.

And, soon enough, he felt the full strength of the sun beating down on him. Warming up his anorak. Drying him out.

The gloom rolled back from the village up ahead, and, for the first time, Bert could truly appreciate Phardoe.

Well . . . after a cursory glance over the place, Bert had to admit that he was a touch disappointed at what he saw, which wasn't to say that he *was* disappointed.

Perhaps *weathered* might've been a better turn of phrase.

Yes, that would do.

The gist of the thing was that Phardoe, right down to the wire hanging baskets bearing flowers of various jolly summer colours: cherry reds, and verdant greens, and banana yellows . . . if bananas could stretch to being a 'summer' colour . . . was pretty much a straight facsimile of Earknork.

Maybe disappointment *was* the right word for it . . . but Bert reminded himself that this was the first village he had only gone and stridden out to and so he should really do his best to make the most of it.

To *suck* up all that he could.

The path beneath his feet soon transformed to cobblestones —an awful lot like Earknork did—and he soon experienced the signs of industry about the town, the gnomes that weren't running their confidence tricks about town, the ones that he often termed the Honest Folk: the bakers, and the carpenters, and the cooks . . .

For some reason, he found himself being swept away by that

last one, maybe it had something to do with the hearty, buttery smell of mushroom soup carrying on the air.

Yes, that was most likely it.

It was almost as if those smells ebbed through the air and massaged his rosy red cheeks: naturally rosy but now all the more so owing to the trek he'd just made along the mountainous . . . okay, really, it was more like a little bit *hilly* . . . path.

Almost of its own accord, his nose led him along the pleasant cobbled streets, along past the flawless cream, plaster-coated cottages, all with their window frames and doors painted the same jolly summer colours as the flowers in the hanging baskets.

He breathed in the smells of roses and of vermillion and of posies, and he couldn't help feeling that familiar tingle within his nostrils and that tightness in his chest: the same one he always got when he had to go visit Earknork on some errand.

For all its similarity to Earknork, Bert had to admit that one of the nicer aspects of Phardoe was that it felt just like *home*.

But, now, to that mushroom soup!

A SOLID LUNCH

I F THERE WAS one thing that Bert was specifically terrific at, it was sniffing out home-cooked food . . . which was really to say that he was good at sniffing out food that he could exchange for money . . . or, to put it yet another way, food that he had to exert no effort to cook himself.

His nose led him off down a back alley, pleasantly named Primrose Pass, and he found himself staring up at the curly-lettered sign which read: *Ma'am Mears's Mayble Pastries*.

He was a little disappointed that the alliteration couldn't stretch to a fourth word, but he was willing to forgive grammar for a moment, so lost was he in the buttery odour seeping out of the place. So thick in the air that it was almost as if he simply needed to take a chomp right here and now and he would be satisfied.

It wasn't *quite* like that, though, and it turned out that he had to push his way on in through the pale-blue door off *Ma'am Mears's*, see his way past the steamed-up windows, and onto a stool which stood at an oak counter.

He sat there staring into the open-plan kitchen inside. It was fairly tight, *cosy* was what more polite gnomes might've called it. He turned his attention quite quickly to the bubbling-away pots on the stoves there. And the steam which jetted on out from all of them.

Pumping marvellous smells into the air.

Salivating didn't *begin* to explain the thing.

It was like his mouth had suddenly decided that right here, in *Ma'am Mears's*, might be a decent place to start out an ocean.

Bert swallowed back the last of his saliva-inflected fudge, then spoke loud and proud, saying, ". . . Um, hello?"

There was no response to his greeting. Unless the continuing bubbling of pots and the consistent pouring of steam could be counted.

And since those, even throughout Gnomelandia, were fairly considered to be inanimate objects, they really couldn't.

He drummed his fingers on the counter, feeling his stomach quiver a little harder, that sensation that, down in his mine, he'd learned to recognise as a need to shove a fresh few palmfuls of fudge past his lips.

Time to try again.

". . . Ma'am . . . Ma'am Mears's?"

Bubbling pots.

Pouring steam.

Not a lot else.

That thick, sweet, buttery mushroom soup flavour seemed to

be congealing in the air now, tempting him down off his stool and over to the pot—to go grab himself a ladle and spoon himself some mushroom soup fresh out of the pot, and manners be damned . . . which was to say nothing of the exchange of money.

He decided that it was one more go and then he simply couldn't resist any more.

"Hello?"

No reply. Yet again.

Sucking in his gut, in an attempt to keep it from rumbling, Bert eased himself down off his stool and into the archway which led into the kitchen.

For a second or so, he just stood there, completely paralysed by the intensity of the smells. It was true what they said about walking building up an appetite. He could feel his hunger right down to the very base of his stomach.

He glanced about, as if Ma'am Mears's might've constructed this whole thing as a test, and that she was just watching on over his shoulder. Waiting for him to make the fatal mistake that would mean she could call the police. Have this unseemly *vagrant* tossed into a cell for a few hours.

But there was still no one in sight.

And so, throwing caution to the wind, Bert stepped up to the most promising-looking pot, the one which had its lid bouncing up off it, and he slipped it away.

There, inside the pot, the thick, creamy mushroom soup bubbled about, just begging him to take a swig of it . . . if it could really be said that any food really desires to be eaten at all, though, at that point philosophical considerations were the least of Bert's thoughts.

He encountered that long-imagined wooden ladle, lying carelessly down on the wooden kitchen counter. He snatched it up and then dunked it into the soup just as quickly. Gave it a quick stir and then brought the boiling hot soup up to his nose.

A sniff, for smell, and a blow, to cool, later he felt the warm soup pumping down his throat, heating him up from the inside.

He set the ladle back inside the pot, looked about again, surely *now* expecting Ma'am Mears's to be looking over his shoulder, dressed in her pinny, brandishing a rolling pin in her intimidating, hammy fists.

But no. No one there.

And so Bert set his mind to scouting out the rest of the kitchen. Found some delicious bread, just at that perfect cooling-off temperature, and he ate that too. Once he'd got done with the bread, he came across a frothy churn of hot chocolate which he, rather cheekily, he thought, tipped out into a waiting wooden mug and had not only seconds of, but thirds too.

All full-up, Bert turned his mind to his journey once again.

He produced his billfold from the inside of his anorak, peeled off a few notes, gave them a quick wipe on his trousers in an attempt to get them in some sort of dry state, and then he laid them down on the wooden counter.

He thought about writing out a note of thanks too, but realised that he hadn't brought a quill along with him.

But he thought the money would be understood just fine.

When he emerged outside, out into Phardoe, back to those cobbled streets stained in drizzle, he couldn't help thinking that the place seemed awfully empty.

Deserted even.

But, no, that wasn't quite it. That didn't *quite* capture just what he was experiencing.

Because it was a special sort of desertedness.

It was *recently* deserted.

ONWARDS

G ENERAL ARDULL munched a little harder on his yaltas leaves, feeling that throbbing, woozy sensation taking hold of his muscles, numbing him right down to his blood. He was getting a taste for the fairly monotonous, leafy flavour of the yaltas, and, he had to admit, if only to himself, just a touch addicted.

Why, just this morning, he'd woken up in cold sweats, shaking all over. And he'd only realised just why his hands were shaking so much when he'd found himself, subconsciously, reaching for his pouch of yaltas.

Even just giving them a sniff had placated him somewhat—at least taken the edge of his shaking.

A little worrying, perhaps.

Still, drugs and armies, the two went together fairly inevitably.

How else was he to keep his troops, *himself*, well motivated in the face of what, by some accounts, could quite easily be described as 'wicked' deeds?

Ardull led the front of his column, his loping troops, boots crunching along the hardening ground, all of them grasping their rifles, keeping them pointed up in the air.

This morning there'd been a fairly unpleasant incident when one of his soldiers, apparently getting a little slack, had shot another in his bottom.

Though Ardull had had no conclusive, concrete evidence to present, he was fairly certain that the shooting had had to do with a card game that'd stretched long into the night before.

Ardull had said nothing about the game, or those boisterous bellows that'd come from the tent. He knew that his gnomes needed to let their hair and beards down at some time or other, and that was all that they'd been doing.

But the issue with these card games was that, inevitably, someone got their feelings hurt or, worse, their money taken.

Yes, that was the thing with their tribe, with those from Juttle, that way that honour overrode just about everything. And how honesty rode high above all else.

The only conclusion that Ardull could draw from that game last night, and the subsequent shooting that morning, was that one of the soldiers had, no doubt, been caught out cheating.

And so getting shot in the bottom was probably just about the measure of what he deserved.

That was pretty much how Ardull's belief in leadership went.

He'd learned that gnomes under command had a good sense of justice, and how to attain it, within themselves.

Ardull's role, as he saw it, was merely just to point out where they should get themselves marching and to have them break for mealtimes.

As Ardull paced along, making a point to keep his arms firmly down at his sides . . . no writhing his hands at the base of his back as if he was an elderly gnome on an evening perambulation . . . he could hear the gentle pants of asthma of his personal assistant, Jeorge.

He had no need to glance back over his shoulder to know that it was Jeorge. Jeorge's breathing was that distinctive. He knew that he'd see that pudgy face, those unlikely bushy brown eyebrows, and that caterpillar-like moustache clinging for dear life to the poor boy's upper lip as if it was some sort of miserable attempt to show some sort of machismo.

The smell of Jeorge's sweat, too, constantly drooling out of his skin, was a dead giveaway.

Ardull scanned the horizon: green and leafy now, those very nice-looking rolling hills, with just the odd tree about here and there. That was fine. He was happy with just the odd tree. But those forests, those *jungles* where they'd picked up the yaltas, goodness, they really had been a trek and a half.

He hoped that the Dwinns would be something of an easier stroll . . . though he couldn't help wondering, although they still had several bags full of them, whether or not there might be some more yaltas waiting for them there.

Fresh off the tree, that would be . . .

"Sir? Sir?" Jeorge said, making walking and talking seem much more difficult than it looked.

"Hmm?" Ardull replied.

"Got news back from the scouts."

Ardull thought it over. He had almost forgotten that late last night, as some sort of an inkling, though he wasn't sure why it'd occurred to him given their knowledge of the Dwinns and their total inaction when it came to defence, he had told Jeorge to form a scouting group to go and check out the road ahead.

Still, it had been a worthwhile move, and one which, Ardull had hoped, would guard them from any kind of arrogance.

After all, there was no such thing as underestimating an *enemy*.

"And?" Ardull said.

"It seems, um, from the news that they've passed onto me, that they were spotted by some watchtowers, or something."

Ardull jerked his head back. Actually looked to Jeorge. There was no need, really, though, since he was just how he'd imagined in his mind's eye.

Camos droopy off his chubby frame, and his cheeks all pink and exerted.

Those frown lines ever-present on his brow.

"And?" Ardull said.

Jeorge's eyes bulged from their sockets. "Well, we believe that the Dwindians might've rumbled us—they might know that something's up, that they're about to be under attack."

Ardull kept up his march, and turned his attention back to their destination, back to those greens up ahead. Their promised land. To this place that was just ripe for the taking.

Had he made a mistake, though?

Would he have been better off not having sent out those scouts last night?

He heaved his shoulders and gave a deep belly sigh.

There was nothing to be done now, of course, they'd only

have to trust the intel they'd gathered before setting out on this trip.

The Dwinns was defenceless and ripe for the taking.

Arrive and Occupy.

That was the whole deal.

And that was right where Ardull's brief ended too.

So, stamping a conscious full-stop on these worries, he marched on harder, listening to Jeorge's asthmatic breathing slowly fade at his heels as he fell behind.

. . . Just hearing Jeorge fall behind, getting to thinking about all the marching ahead of them, got Ardull's mind straight back onto the yaltas, and that, he knew, was a slippery slope indeed.

QUIET, TOO QUIET

BERT SCOUTED out the whole of Phardoe trying to make some sort of sense of the deserted village. He didn't have to do that on an empty stomach, though, of course, and he successfully scouted out a bakery which had some of the most delicious lemon drizzle cake he'd ever tasted.

Once he'd polished off his sixth slice . . . it really was *very* light . . . he stood on the doorstep of the bakery licking the stickiness off his fingers and wondering whether he might be able to score some fudge anywhere about the place.

He'd brought plenty along with him, of course, but it never hurt to have an abundance.

Where fudge was concerned, you could *never* have too much.

As he stood in the doorway of the bakery, the warmth from the ovens on his back, and the chilly breeze sneaking on through the cobbled streets fresh on his cheeks, he thought he could hear footsteps.

Since he'd now spent an hour or more in Phardoe without so much as seeing a soul, he didn't get his hopes up, reminding himself that the place was deserted.

Most likely this was an aural hallucination, and he knew how to recognise them too, since he would have plenty when he was working down the mine.

Was he hearing one now, though?

He truly couldn't say for sure.

Those footsteps sounded very real to him.

And so he took the initiative, clinging tight to the strap of his rucksack and making off in the direction of the sound.

The trail brought him to the centre of the town—again, very much like Earknork—which consisted of a lightly spraying fountain, and a statue of the founding gnome of the place, apparently Phardoe's namesake.

Bert always found that a ridiculous ego move to name a town after yourself, and it got on his nerves that even his own Earknork was named after the founder.

Nothing to do now, though, considering the place had been founded, and *named*, a solid thousand or more years ago.

He breathed in the fresh air of the place, that mountain air that blew down over the town . . . again, much like it did in Earknork.

He guessed that he'd always said to himself that the Dwinns wasn't exactly a hotbed of imagination or outside-the-box thinking.

As Bert strolled on to the other side of the centre of town, he caught sight of someone.

A flash of clothing. Nothing more.

Strangely, Bert felt his heart give a slight leap in his chest, felt his blood quicken about his veins. He had never really had trouble with loneliness, or at least he'd always told himself that he was better off on his own pretty much always, but now he certainly felt a rush of excitement he couldn't ever have imagined feeling while alone.

He made off in the direction of the gnome, catching another sight of their clothing.

A silver-grey colour.

He listened to the rubber soles of his wellies squeaking against the soaked cobblestones as he went. And, dizzy and at the back of his mind, he hoped that he wouldn't slip over and crack his skull open.

Luckily he didn't.

But he *did* lose sight of the gnome.

And ended up staring at a dead-end alley.

Just a bunch of shuttered-up doors and windows for company.

The sun chose that moment, for some reason, to start *really* shining overhead.

Bert felt the warmth of the rays on his anorak, felt it warming his blood even more, following up on the sensation he'd had on seeing that gnome out ahead of him.

He stood his ground and waited, thinking over his next move.

He had to get a wiggle on, of course. He needed to make for the Gnomish Council of the Dwinns. But, at the same time, he found himself racked with intrigue at just what had gone on here, in this town. As to why this whole place was totally deserted . . . and its food so delicious.

Just as Bert was on the brink of turning on his heel, of

heading back off into town, and then back out the other side of it, he watched a rusty-brown drain cover, in the midst of the cobblestones, lift up a couple of inches. Saw a pair of eyes staring out from within the gloom.

Bert just blinked a little, trying to bring this image straight before him. Trying to make his brain believe that he was actually seeing what he was seeing.

When the eyes wandered over him, the drain cover soon dropped again with a *clang* of metal on stone.

Bert broke from his daze and stepped on over to the drain cover.

It was actually quite easy to prise it open, which was to say that there was an extremely convenient pop-up metal handle that Bert had only to flip out of its bedding and give a good old tug.

The drain cover lifted up. Not that heavy. At least not as heavy as a whole wheelbarrow of excavated rocks.

He stared on down there, to the gnome staring back up at him, his eyes a light-green colour, and glinting just a little in the sun.

"Hello," Bert said.

CROWDED ALL OF A SUDDEN?

THE OTHER GNOME, who had tight, youthful skin, and wore what Bert now saw were silver-grey *overalls*, seemed a little taken aback for a long while. He also had flame-red hair that shimmied a little in direct sunlight.

"Do you, uh," Bert continued, "speak at all?"

The other gnome blinked once, twice, and then said, ". . . Yes, I speak."

"Ah, good," Bert said, giving him his best stranger's smile.

Then he glanced about himself, about the alley they found themselves down as if worried that someone might be watching —that whoever it was that this gnome was clearly hiding from might be bearing down on him too.

There was no one, though.

He turned his attention back to the cowering gnome in the storm drain. "Uh, any reason that there's nobody about town today?"

46

The gnome stared up at him, eyes wide and clearly panicked. "They're coming."

"Who's coming?"

"You . . . you haven't heard?"

Bert thought about it a moment, then decided he hadn't.

He shook his head.

The gnome blinked another dozen or so times in rapid succession, then said, "The scouts on the frontiers say that there's a great big movement of gnomes coming—*soldiers*." He drew a snatched breath. "That they think that they're coming to *conquer* us."

"And they won't be able to conquer you down in that drain?"

The gnome seemed confused for a couple of moments, and then he broke out into an uneasy smile. "I . . . I couldn't think of any other place to hide." He swallowed hard, and Bert watched the gnome's Adam's apple bob in his throat. "Everyone evacuated, see? They all headed on off."

"Where to?" Bert said.

The gnome shrugged. "I told you I wasn't about for it, didn't I?"

"Don't think you did."

"Oh, well, I wasn't about for it."

Bert felt his back tweaking from all this bending over. He guessed that a lifetime of independent mining did that to a gnome. Sometimes it was difficult to imagine that he wasn't a ninety-year-old anymore.

"What're you planning on doing now, then?" Bert said.

The gnome's eyes darted about. "Uh, I . . . I hadn't got that far. To be honest, I thought you were one of those *bad* gnomes,

47

one of the ones that'd come here to conquer us, so I just thought I'd better hide out as quickly as I could."

"That sounds reasonable enough."

The gnome gave a sigh. "No, no," he said, his voice getting quieter as he spoke. "Really, I've always been a coward—I think that's just my personality, maybe it's genetic even. I think I remember my father being a coward, my grandfather too."

The gnome rested his fingers in the pit of his chin, as if deep in thought, but before he could blabber on anymore, Bert saw fit to step in.

"Listen," Bert said, "if we can't track down any of your fellow villagers then what would you think of coming along with me?"

"Why?" the gnome said, looking a little startled for no particular reason, "What've I got that you need?"

Bert was a little taken aback by the directness of the question. Though he guessed that it was a good one. "Oh, well, you look like you might be . . ." the word he was looking for was 'good company,' but instead he settled on ". . . *useful.*"

"Useful?" the gnome said, sounding deeply suspicious, and then, his voice rising in pitch, "*Useful? Me?*"

"Yeah, I mean, you're dressed in overalls, what's your trade?"

The gnome glared about himself, and then looked down at his overalls, pinching the fabric between his thumb and forefinger. As if he'd just remembered the question, he glanced back up at Bert and said, "I'm a, uh, a blacksmith."

"See?" Bert said. "That's useful."

The gnome furrowed his brow. "What, you're planning on taking a furnace along with you on this . . . this *quest* of yours?"

"Quest?" Bert said, not having thought of what he was doing as that before . . . but now he did, he had to admit that it sort of made sense . . . it was a quest insomuch as he had something that he needed to get done, and a place to go and get that something done *in*.

"Hmm," the gnome replied.

"Well," Bert said, "I hadn't planned on taking a furnace along, but—"

"Then just what use would *I* be?"

Bert decided that now it was better to change tack. Better for him just to tell this gnome that, really, what he *really* longed for on this 'quest' was a bit of company.

But, and maybe this was just his dishonest Dwindian gnome genes peeping up to say hello, he settled on, "Well, you're better off with me than stalking about this place, all deserted, waiting for those *bad* gnomes to come."

The gnome seemed to consider this for another few seconds. His eyes shifting about their sockets as he did so, as if somewhere there, behind the scenes, inside his brain, his eyes had to physically sift through the options all presented to him.

Then, with a faint sigh, the gnome said, "Okay then, you've sold me."

"What's your name?" Bert said.

The gnome slowly turned his eyes onto his, and then said, in a doleful, almost regretful tone, "Uglax."

Uglax.

An interesting name.

A *memorable* name, at the very least.

And a name that sounded, to Bert, very much like 'friend.'

THE FRONTIER

B Y HIS INTRINSIC GNOME SENSE, Ardull knew that
it was around midday by the time they brought the frontier between Poot and the Dwinns into sight. And the watchtowers soon followed.

Ardull ordered his gnomes to stand by, for them all to grasp
their rifles and to be ready for any sudden strike. A well-aimed
sniper shot, perhaps, from one of those watchtowers.

Nothing came, however, and Ardull felt the confidence
flowing thicker and warmer with every step he took, leading his
gnomes along on the trudge towards the frontier.

Or maybe the confidence was coming more from the yaltas
that he was chain-chewing, and which he had begun to worry
desperately about the stocks of.

When he'd checked over the supplies, he'd found that they
were down to the last couple of sacks of yaltas leaves.

The demand for the yaltas had surprised even Ardull, and he

couldn't help worrying that the stocks they had with them wouldn't last much longer than a day at most.

Ardull stepped through the long grass and to the base of the first watchtower.

It was made of thick, wooden logs, and had a roof made up entirely of rushes.

It was also totally deserted.

There wasn't a Dwindian in sight.

All the better.

Ardull glanced over his shoulder, to his gnomes as they snaked their way up the hillside behind him. Then he brought them to a halt. They deserved a rest.

Looking down the crest of the hill, down the other side and into the Dwinns Domain, he could see that it was all a downward slope.

The end was in sight.

All they'd need to do was capture the administrative capital, wherever that was, and declare the Dwinns annexed under the power of Juttle.

Juttilians would rule these lands for years to come, Ardull was sure of it.

He might even manage to get them to name one of the captured towns after himself.

That kind of thing had always had a habit of tickling his fancy, though he did recognise that it was a bit of an ego-stroke too.

But who didn't need their ego stroking once in a while?

His gnomes slouched about, bringing out their rations, and chatting about themselves.

Ardull was a little anxious upon seeing one of them overturn a box of supplies to be used as a card table. He had often thought about banning card games on his watch, but had decided against it, citing morale as the obvious upside of these card games.

And as long as they didn't graduate from shooting one another in the backside, Ardull had to admit that he really couldn't see the harm in the games.

He strode on down the hillside, behind the dozen or so watchtowers, consciously taking his first step into Dwindian territory. He breathed the air. Found that it tasted much the same, if perhaps just a touch, and this was a bit of a far-out claim, but what the hell . . . mountainy?

Yes, that same fresh sort of crisp, icy wind that came off snow-capped mountains.

Or just off frost-plastered hilltops.

That was all part of the adventure, him and his troops going off to discover just what the Dwinns had in store for them.

As Ardull enjoyed the brisk silence, and the clean air, he dipped his hand into his pocket, feeling for the crunched-up, dusty remains of his yaltas.

He snatched them up between his fingers and then stuffed them in between his lips.

They were all dried up and clearly the dregs of the bag, but he got that same familiar buzz out of chewing them so he made a point not to complain too much.

After he'd got them all chewing in his mouth, he gave the bag a good sniff.

He really couldn't say what it was about the smell of the yaltas . . . it wasn't like they smelled any different from any other leaves, and yet he had to admit that something about it was extremely . . . *moreish.*

He heard the asthmatic panting and smelled the pork-chop sweat of Jeorge approaching at his elbow. Ardull kept his eyes on the horizon, on those fuzzy, blue-green mountains, the Dwinns all spread out ahead.

"Hmm?" Ardull said, finally acknowledging his assistant.

"How long will we break here, sir?"

"What?"

"I mean, are we going to put up camp here—on the frontier?"

Ardull glanced back at him. Shook his head. He gave a faint smile. "Oh no, I don't think so. We must strike while the iron is hot—we need to continue our march onwards into enemy territory. We cannot allow the enemy the luxury of preparation now that they may well have caught wind of our presence here."

"Very well, sir," Jeorge said, his eyes dipping down to the toes of his boots, no doubt having wished for a longish break here.

Ardull rolled his eyes and turned back to the green landscape. It was like a cloth all draped across a table. A *green* tablecloth.

Yes, that was it.

He dug about inside his jacket, and removed his spiral-ring notebook, the one that he used for his poetic scribblings. He aimed a glance back over his shoulder at Jeorge, and Jeorge, well trained to the cue, breathed out a deep sigh and trudged away from him.

Ardull licked the nib of his pencil and surveyed the lands, and then, keeping his hand steady, he wrote out the steady verses, so that his wife would easily be able to make out the letters later on when she received it—so that she wouldn't make a mistake as she transcribed his words into her flowery, *woman's* hand for his *Grand Compendium of Poetical Musings*.

He recalled when his wife had claimed that 'Poetical' wasn't a word, and he'd had to assure her that it was.

And, anyway, if it wasn't who cared?

Poets floated on the breeze and . . . uh, scribbled with their quills.

They could *invent* whichever word suited their needs!

Ardull flipped the page of his notebook. Pressed his pencil to the page and wrote:

> The green fields flow,
> From out beneath,
> They do bequeath,
> The passing time,
> And the battle to be fought.

Ardull leaned back from his notebook, as he liked to do to better get a look at his work.

Yes, this was a good start, and one which would inspire him all the more.

Which he would surely transform into a masterpiece.

He pocketed his notebook and looked down, over the land before him again.

The Dwinns.

It would soon belong to the Juttilian Domain.

HIDE AND SEEK

BERT, along with his new companion, Uglax, who insisted that he shorten his name to 'Lax' which Bert, on balance, supposed was better than 'Ug,' headed on through the town, looking for any sign of life, or even so much as an indication of just where the occupants had fled too.

But there was nothing.

Chewing away at a fresh, and extremely sugary, wad of fudge lodged into his molars, Bert squatted over and studied the spot at the edge of town where the cobblestones ceased and the fallow lands took off.

He saw several footprints left marked in the earth, but since they headed off in both directions, both away from the village, and towards it, they didn't give much of a hint as to where the gnomes had fled.

He straightened up, took in a whole lungful of that fresh

mountain air—air that, although he had breathed it just about every one of his days on earth, he would never tire of.

He heard it whistle in through the valleys, and make the long grasses all go *swoosh*.

He held his anorak in his arms, wrapped there, since the sun had brought a little warmth along with it. He eyed Lax in those green eyes of his and said, "No idea at all about where they've headed off to?"

Lax shook his head.

Bert gave a sigh and then collected himself together, reasoning that, really, it didn't matter all that much where the occupants of the town had gone. The pressing business was this army of gnomes that Lax had mentioned.

That was what they should look out for.

He looked about the village, trying to find some sort of direction. He looked up to the sky, to the position of the sun, and calibrated it with his gnome sense of time—an old farmer's trick. And then he recalled that he'd brought a compass with him, and he dug it out of his pocket, pointed it off due east, and made for that direction.

He only noticed that Lax wasn't following after a good thirty paces. It was when he looked back and saw him standing there looking thoroughly useless in his silver-grey overalls, with his flame-red hair, and his pale skin.

"What's the matter?" Bert called to him.

Lax didn't respond. He stayed in his place. His eyes meeting Bert's.

Bert felt another sigh coming along and then he told himself not to be such an insensitive oaf. He'd already kicked a dog down a steep valley on this quest—albeit a *rabid* one—so making an adolescent cry wouldn't be exactly doing his case any good at all with the gods . . . if *they* even existed at all.

Bert thought it better not to think too hard about it.

But sometimes he did get to thinking through things like that in the gloom of the mine.

Nothing much else to think about down there, once you'd got through with all the lady-gnome fantasies, in any case.

Bert took a couple of steps back towards Lax, the brass compass still clasped in his palm, and duly pointing north in that faithful way that compasses always do.

"Eh?" Bert said, letting his hand holding the compass fall away down at his side.

Now that he'd closed in on the distance between him and Lax, he saw that Lax was crying. No, that wasn't the word for it. It was more like *bawling*.

Tears ran down his cheeks in rivulets, and sparkled in the sunlight.

"You're crying," Bert said.

Lax's eyes were all puffed-up and dopey-looking too, but Bert thought it was better not to say anything about that.

There was only so much stating the obvious he could do for one day.

Bert wondered what he was supposed to do. He hadn't really encountered much in the way of gnomic interaction, certainly nothing like this. Seeing as his workplace consisted of big hunks of rock and darkness. Down in his mine he encountered nothing like an actual gnome *crying*. Not even himself. To be honest, crying had never really occurred to him as a viable thing to consider doing.

. . . But, wait, his housekeeper, Tilda, he remembered now!

Yes, one day, after he'd skimped off early from the mine—and, hey, why shouldn't he, what with him being the boss and all?—he'd got in through the front door to his home, to his mansion, to hear sniffling.

At first he was sure that a pipe somewhere in the house had sprung a leak and that it was spitting boiling-hot water, streamed right in from a mountain thermal, all about the place.

But once Bert had taken a few more footsteps into his house, heard the *thud-thud* of his footsteps resounding about the marble floors of the front hall, swallowed his celebratory fudge down, his mouth still warmed by the sugar, he had suddenly realised just what was going on.

That Tilda was *crying*.

He had almost doubled back, headed on back up the slope to the mine, to feign like he hadn't even come home at all, and he probably would have done if he hadn't caught her eye as he'd taken his next step forwards.

Seen her in the kitchen.

Hands clutching one of her cleaning rags.

Squatted over.

Sobbing her eyes out.

He scoured his mind for what he'd done then. He could remember, quite clearly, the wonderful smell of a baking chocolate cake. And he recalled that he was fantasising about the sugary icing that would soon go on top when she'd sort of, well . . . yes . . . she'd just thrown herself at him, landed with her cotton-wool hair flat up against his chest.

He'd wanted to tell her that, if she really needed a cuddle, it'd be better for him to go and change into fresh clothes, what with him being covered in stone dust and all.

But he just hadn't been able to say a word.

He'd just felt her pressed up against his chest. Her tears soaking into his soiled tunic.

And he'd . . . yes, that was what he'd done! . . . he'd put his arms about her, hugged her to him . . . and, a little while later, what'd seemed like a solid few hours later in fact, he'd let her go.

And she'd been fine from then on.

Or, well, she'd done a little more sniffling but she'd more or less tugged herself back together.

With a couple of blinks, Bert was back to the present, staring down the twin barrels of those glittering green eyes of Lax's.

Knowing vaguely what to do now, Bert took another few steps, over into him, and, gently, feeling the hair on his arms rising up, he embraced the boy.

Hugged him to his chest.

?

BERT FIRST got the impression that something was up when he felt Lax pushing hard back at him. Felt his hands shoving him somewhere about the collarbone.

Shoving him *away*.

Bert clung on for a fair few seconds but then decided that he'd be better off giving this thing up. After all, however titch this blacksmith looked, he was probably packing some significant strength on account of his job.

He knew how muscles had a habit of knotting all up and looking all weedy till the moment they struck—he *was* a miner after all.

When they got to be about a shoulder's length apart, Bert noticed Lax scowling at him, his eyes now pretty much dry of tears. But his eyes still puffy.

"Wha . . . what?" Lax said, apparently not quite able to put whatever he wanted to say into words.

Bert thought that right now wasn't a good time for a smile. So he just settled for a little nervous scratching of his arm. "I . . . uh, well, you see . . ."

Lax widened his eyes. "You were trying to . . . to . . ."

"It's just," Bert said, snapping into action, wanting to settle this awkward matter, "I thought you were upset, that's all, and I thought I could, uh . . . *comfort* you, you know?"

"By . . . by, hugging me?"

Bert could see just where this discussion was heading and he decided, in the name of efficiency, to see it off early—to nip it in the bud right now.

"So, you, uh, weren't crying then?"

Lax's eyes got wider still. "I have *allergies*," he said. "Coming out here, to the long grasses, all of it gets up my nose, see?" He tilted his head back and flared his nostrils as if this demonstration would clear up all the confusion.

Bert decided that this was a good out. "Yes, yes," he said. "I think I can."

Lax allowed his chin to drop down to his chest. He wouldn't meet Bert's eye, and Bert noticed him, more than once, glancing back over his shoulder as if he was considering the possibility of beating a hasty retreat for the village.

No, it looked like Bert *would* have to *really* see this thing off head-on. "I'm not," he started, "I mean, I'm not . . . you know, of that gnomish persuasion."

Lax narrowed his eyes. ". . . Persuasion?"

"You know, what with you being a blacksmith, that was . . . uh, no . . . what I mean to say is that I, uh, do *not* have any *romantic*, what's it? . . . You understand me?"

Lax didn't look like he did.

Time to change the subject, it seemed.

Bert eyed up the path ahead, the beaten-down trail of long grass leading up another hill. "Look," he said, "we've got to head on out to see the Dwindian Council, this matter's far more urgent now, I mean, if there's anyone who's got the resources to do anything about this . . . this"—it was difficult to speak with what had just happened between them still on his mind, but he decided he was better off just powering through—"these *bad* gnomes."

Lax didn't meet his eye, but he did look off in the direction of the path that led on over the hill which overlooked the village. ". . . Yes," he said, not sounding terribly convincing.

To be fair to Lax, Bert wasn't making an awful lot of sense.

"Look," Bert said, trying again to shine a little logic onto things here, "you're perfectly free to, you know, just hobble on back there—to the village. That's fine. Totally, completely fine. Just, uh, just go back if you'd like to." He looked on ahead to the path. "But I'm going off to see the Council, something has to be done about this whole mess."

Lax screwed up his features and seemed to be thinking over this matter quite hard now.

And perhaps not without good reason.

Bert felt his breath stick in his throat, and it was only then that he recalled the fudge mashed up between his molars and the inside of his cheek.

With a flick of the tongue, he brought it back into the mix and chewed on it a little more, got some more of that sugar into his bloodstream to calm him a little. He squeezed the strap of his knapsack, and listened to the wind still blowing about the hills surrounding the town. When he'd counted to about a hundred in his head, he decided that now was the time to expedite the decision-making process. "Well?" he said.

Lax turned his gaze back over him, then said, "You got a tent with you?"

Bert shook his head.

"Then where're you planning on camping out on the way to the Council?"

"I . . . I hadn't thought about that," Bert said.

Lax jerked his thumb over his shoulder. "Tell you what, back there, back in the village, why don't we go and stock up properly on the stuff we need? You're probably missing other things too. Do you have a gas stove?"

"A gas stove?"

"Yeah, for cooking things?"

"I, uh, I've got a few sandwiches." For some reason Bert thought it would be a good idea to smile. "Ham and cheese if you like them."

"How many?" Lax said, cocking his head to one side.

"Uh, two or three."

"That's not going to last."

"Oh," Bert said.

"You don't really know what you're doing, do you?"

Bert shook his head.

With a smile, Lax waved Bert on to follow him back to the village. "Come on, we'll pick up all the stuff we need." He paused a moment then said, "You've got money, right?"

"Oh yes," Bert said, grinning. "Plenty."

"Good," Lax said, "because I've never believed in stealing."

As Bert followed Lax on back towards the village, he thought about how he was getting to like this kid more and more.

And no, not in *that* way.

ALL STOCKED UP AND READY TO QUEST

I T WAS ABOUT three o'clock in the morning, Bert sensed, when he found himself thanking his lucky stars for having run into Lax, and having brought him along for the ride.

Back in Phardoe they'd picked up a pair of tents, a gas stove, along with a couple of gas cylinders, and some bags of food.

Bert had left money for it all, of course.

For when—*if*—the villagers returned.

The wind howled up against the canvas of Bert's tent. And he watched the material whip about in the sheets of rain. It turned out that the route to the Council was somewhat exposed to the elements. He shuddered, literally, to think how things might've turned out if he hadn't brought a tent along with him.

But, as it had turned out, they'd had a very nice dinner of baked beans with cheese sprinkled over the top. Lax had cooked and Bert hadn't even had to pay him to do so.

That was something different.

Because, and Bert felt himself hoping just a little that he was right, Lax was turning quite swiftly into a good friend though they had only known one another a matter of hours, and their ages were probably a good century apart.

They'd also managed to get their hands on some sleeping bags, inside one of which Bert now lay, with the fuzzy cloth up against his bare skin . . . he liked to sleep naked.

Bert was chewing on his night-time fudge, feeling that same slick, soppy mulch all churning about in the pit of his mouth. It was a good thing that one of the best parts of being a gnome was having teeth of a diamond-like hardness and resistance. Tooth decay just didn't feature when you spent almost your entire life chomping through rock. Dentist bills neither.

Bert wondered about the day ahead of them.

It turned out that, despite his young years, only being around forty, or fifty years old, Lax had done some serious travelling about these parts, which was to say that he seemed to know the route to the Council well enough.

Lax had been the one who, earlier in the day, had insisted that they deviate from Bert's due-east route, to take a safer, faster route down through the valley.

And Bert had trusted him.

He had no reason not to.

After all, he *did* consider Lax his friend now, and friends were to be trusted.

Though he was quite comfortable, Bert stayed awake for a good portion of the night, just lying on his back and watching the canvas ceiling of his tent as it caught the tangerine glow of the morning sun.

He only thought to emerge once he heard the toggles of Lax's tent across from him opening. When Bert did glance out, he noticed that Lax had pitched his tent a clear ten, fifteen paces away from his own.

And, as Bert had discovered in the night when he'd got up to go for a pee, Lax had laid the area with dry twigs . . . made a sort of alarm system that would signal to him whenever Bert left his tent.

He guessed that Lax couldn't be too careful with a stranger, because however much Bert wanted them to treat one another like friends, they still had a way to go before the trust flowed both ways.

By the time Bert had suited himself up, tugged on his anorak, and got his expedition kit all ready to go . . . mainly his compass, that was just about the most important thing they had between them . . . he slipped out through the flap of his tent, and joined Lax where he was cooking them up some more of those beans on the gas stove.

Lax gave Bert a sheepish grin, and then turned his attention back to his cooking.

Bert looked about the landscape. It was a beautiful morning. Flawless, blue skies, and only a sprinkling of wispy clouds about. He was certain that they were through the worst of this stormy weather.

With that sour scent of gas thick in his nostrils, he turned to Lax. "You think we'll make the Council today?" he said.

Lax worked a wooden spatula at the beans in the saucepan, keeping them from burning over the gas stove flame. "Depends," he said.

"On what?"

"If the bridge is in."

"What bridge?"

"The one about the town—the whole town is surrounded by a moat, with a river flowing through it. Since we've been having all this weather it might've flooded up over the bridge, might've made it impassable."

"Has that happened before, I mean, when you've gone there before?"

Lax shrugged. "Nah, but I've heard of it happening." He stirred at the beans in the saucepan, and then added, "But it has rained an awful lot the last few days."

Bert looked out over the path which wormed its way off away from where they were camped, and he hoped that things would turn out fine.

If the stories of these *bad* gnomes entering the Dwinns were true then it was imperative that he get to the Council as soon as possible to alert them.

Unless they'd already been alerted.

But, as Bert knew, it was one thing for the Council to be alerted to something, and quite another for them to actually take any sort of action over it.

In fact, he was certain, if he didn't show up there to drive them into action then they would simply let the matter lie.

Bert found himself lost in his plans when Lax called him to breakfast.

It took Bert a fair few moments to drag his eyes away from the horizon, to the very edge of it, where his wondering had taken him off to.

The rich scent of the baked beans brought him back with a

snap, though, and soon enough he felt like he was ready to face the day with a fresh mind.

To do the best he could to save the Dwinns from this enemy they faced.

An enemy he'd tried to warn them about.

THE FIRST OCCUPATION

ARDULL brought his troops along, gestured for them to follow him up the hillside. The long grasses brushed up against the legs of his camo trousers, and he could smell the recently fallen rain everywhere, making the grasses damp.

That wonderful, fresh smell.

Like everything had been renewed.

The more he saw of the Dwinns, the more he had to admit that he loved it.

This place was a wondrous, temperate climate. Green hills, and sloping valleys. Gushing rivers of fresh, mountain spring water. Crystal clear.

It'd be very easy to get used to this.

He knew, down the other side of this hillside was one of the first villages of the Dwinns. That they could easily take it before nightfall. If they showed discipline. If they were professional.

If they kept on chewing their yaltas leaves.

Just like Ardull was himself.

He had a fresh pouch nestled in the breast pocket of his jacket. The last one. He'd had every soldier issued with one leaf each. After they'd got through with this lot that would be the end of the leaves. If they wanted more they'd have to hot tail it all the way back to Poot, back to the jungles where they'd snaffled them from.

And Ardull couldn't say that the thought hadn't crossed his mind.

Only the goals that he'd been set back in Juttle kept him from turning his gnomes around to go and fetch some more of those leaves.

He'd promised himself, once they'd got control of this, the first village of the Dwinns, he'd send off a crack unit to go and bring back more leaves for the whole of his troop.

Ardull shoved a fresh batch of leaves past his lips, chewed on them. He couldn't believe that he had ever got it into his head before that the leaves were tasteless. Nothing could've been further from the truth. It was quite the opposite. They seemed to carry just about any flavour that he might wish for. He seemed able to project just about any flavour he wished.

Chicken?

Yup.

BBQ ribs?

Also.

Cheesy noodles?

It was almost like he could taste it on his tongue right now.

He listened to his boots as he clambered up the slope. The *squelch* of the mud beneath the rigid treads on his soles. He kept a close watch of his gnomes as they kept level with him.

No one wanting to break over the breach before he'd given the order.

That was how he liked it.

Nice and tight.

Disciplined.

With another chew of the yaltas leaves, he halted, and the rest of his gnomes halted also. They all formed a line, level with him. Just waiting for his order to surge over. To fire their rifles down on any forces that might be awaiting them in the village down below.

His heart ticked on in his eardrums.

He could hear Jeorge's asthmatic breathing in his ear.

Could smell his fishy sweat.

Knew that he was waiting on his orders just as much as the rest of the soldiers were.

They had to wait.

Just another moment.

Everyone had to be in file, and . . .

Ardull brought his arm downwards.

As one, his gnomes swarmed up the slope, rifles in their clutches, all of them readying to squeeze their triggers.

The key behind Arrive and Occupy was the element of surprise, and they certainly had it right here. No, they just needed to press home their advantage, and snuff out any resistance.

He watched the first of his gnomes head on over the top of the hill, eyes fixed to the sight of their rifles, ready to gun anyone down.

He listened for the fair few cracks of warning fire, that call for any gnome on the other side, waiting down there in the village, to think long and hard about surrendering right here and now.

His gnomes cried out as they barrelled on down the valley, unseen to Ardull.

Ardull could still hear Jeorge's breathing thick in his ear, and he wanted to tell him to stop. But he couldn't move a muscle. He was locked in position. All these weeks and months of marching and it had brought them here. To this first village.

Now he would see just how his gnomes stood up in combat.

No more shots followed the warning fire.

Ardull waited out the seconds, but soon allowed himself to get his hopes going—that this would be a bloodless victory.

Just how he liked them.

There was nothing messier than gnome blood.

Ardull crouched down, into the side of the hill, and gently tapped the side of his boot with his thumb, counting the seconds as they passed by, and then, in a moment of pure inspiration, he reached for the inside of his jacket again, withdrew his notebook tucked up inside there.

After the cautionary glare in Jeorge's general direction, and Jeorge scampering off a couple of paces so that he wouldn't be able to peer over his shoulder, Ardull took to writing, to continuing his verse:

> The quiet hill, it waits,
> And the wind blows, waiting also,
> The trees, they stand on duty,
> For the bloodless victory won,
> And fought evermore.

Ardull gave the loop of the 't' on 'fought' an extra special sweep of his hand, so delighted was he with the way the verse had turned out.

After the standard check for legibility, he restored the pencil to the spiral rings of the notebook and tucked it back inside his jacket for safety.

Gods, how he hated war.

And how he *loved* poetry.

THE COUNCIL OF THE DWINNS

BERT FELT his heart pumping hard. Tapping against his ribcage. He could feel the heat rising up to his cheeks. And that faint taste of blood in his mouth, that faint taste he got after a hard day at the mines, one that might have involved a whole bunch of chewing on bedrock.

The trick with bedrock was to give it a good gumming. To get as much saliva coating it as you possibly could. That way, what with gnome saliva working as a kind of acid, it could be bitten into all the easier.

When he breathed in now, he had a slightly musty smell about himself. All this travelling had certainly left its mark on his anorak, which was pretty soaked in sweat following all the exertion.

He listened to the even *crunch* as Lax passed over the path ahead of him, leading the way. He had to admit that the kid set a mean, old pace. One that Bert had been sure he would've been able to keep up with without all that much effort.

He'd always believed that he'd been in great shape, and he did have good biceps, some pretty rock-solid thighs. Seeing as he spent the majority of his life lifting rocks and such that really seemed to follow.

But Lax had showed him that he might have overestimated his abilities—he supposed that the energy of youth could never be underestimated.

Bert pushed on harder, and saw that the top of the hill was coming up. He watched on as Lax stepped on over it, and followed after.

As Bert passed over the top of the hill he saw the town coming into view below.

Steep rooftops, all bent into acute angles. Winding, cobbled streets bustling with activity. Horse and carts, and marketplaces with multi-coloured tarps keeping their vendors sheltered from the fierce sun.

Cormersbarn.

Capital, and the home of the Gnomish Council of the Dwinns.

Home of many letters and recipient of his diligently paid taxes.

And what seemed to Bert just about the most ineffective government in the entire history of gnomedom.

Not that he had done all that much studying on the subject.

Bert considered that he hadn't really known what to expect upon breathing in. He hadn't known just what Cormersbarn would smell like.

But, as it turned out, and as wasn't all that surprising on

reflection, the whole place stank of horse manure . . . and of gnome manure too.

He guessed that was all part and parcel of a town as sprawling as the one laid out below. Why, even standing here, on this hill that overlooked the place, he couldn't see the full extent of the town. The houses bent off over the horizon.

The next thing that struck Bert was to check for the moat about the town.

He saw that it had, like Lax had suggested, burst its banks and now covered the bridges which led out off the plains and into the town.

Next Bert took in the wall which surrounded the whole of the town—made out of sturdy brickwork, and it loomed high above the tallest house's rooftop.

It was only now that Bert wondered just how easy it was going to be to get into the town on a good day, let alone one like today with the moat all flooded.

Bert looked to Lax for answers, but, instead, he got quite a different response.

"They like to close themselves in," Lax said. "That's the whole business about the wall, and the moat. They're probably loving the fact that the moat burst its banks and now no one can either come or go from the town."

"So what do we do? Do you think they've heard the warning —about what's coming?"

Lax shrugged. "Perhaps they might have got news but that won't change what they'll do. These gnomes, the gnomes of Cormersbarn, they think that as long as they're behind their walls and their moat they'll be just fine from any attack possible . . . though, to be honest, I really don't think that they believe anyone would ever *dream* of launching an attack on them."

"Guess it's going to be a rude awakening, then?"

"You could say that," Lax said.

Bert surveyed the place. Tried to work out just what they were going to do next. He had come here for a reason and there was no chance that he was simply going to give up now.

Nor was he going to stand about here like a lemon till the water level in the moat went down far enough for them to chance crossing over into the town.

He had to have his audience with the Council *today*.

He turned to Lax, the question on his lips.

But, before he could pick Lax's brains for what to do, Lax lowered his voice and said in a tone close to a whisper, "I've got a plan."

BREAKING AND ENTERING

B ERT KEPT his knapsack tight to his back as he descended the hill. It was true what Lax had said, about the wall being a way to keep others out of the town. Down at ground level it looked an insurmountable obstacle.

But Lax had assured him that it wasn't the case.

Bert guessed that they would see pretty soon.

The first obstacle they had to clear, of course, was the moat standing before them. It overflowed its banks, and its waters lapped at the long grass of the plains. The water itself was a light-brown colour and it gleamed in the sunlight.

Breathing in now, Bert found the stench of horse manure almost unbearable, so much so that it actually sent his heart racing just to smell it.

As they'd come down the hill, Bert had noticed Lax collecting together tree branches, and, as they'd gone along, he'd worked at threading them together using some technique involving long grass that Bert truly had not a clue about . . . even though he was sure that he'd watched pretty much every movement as he'd made the knots.

Now what Lax held in his hands resembled a kind of ladder.

Just a short, stumpy ladder.

Only about the size and breadth of his chest.

Nothing at all remarkable.

And certainly not sturdy enough for them to use to scale the wall of the town.

Let alone sail across the moat.

Bert looked to Lax in expectation.

So far he'd steered them right, along the right path to reaching the town, so he didn't see why he shouldn't trust in his abilities now.

He wondered just what one learned in the blacksmith trade these days because, everything else aside, it seemed to instil a great amount of pragmatic thinking if Lax was anything to go by.

Lax brought the branches he'd gathered together to the moat and he laid them down on the surface of the water. He held them there, clutching them so tightly that his knuckles turned white from the effort.

Bert drew a deep breath, ready now to see just what Lax had in mind.

Lax's brow wrinkled as he concentrated on the branches he held on the surface of the moat. And then, in a single, smooth action, he let them go.

The branches floated for approximately seven seconds before promptly sinking without a trace.

Bert blinked several times, staring at the bubbles that rose to the surface from where the branches had just sunk away out of sight. Then he turned his attention to Lax, looking to him with expectation.

All Lax had to offer him was a shrug and a, "I thought it would work."

Bert looked back to the place where the branches had sunk.

There weren't even any bubbles rising to the surface anymore.

He guessed that even he, someone he thought of as being an excellent judge of character, could sometimes be completely and utterly wrong.

That was just the way it went sometimes.

Bert looked to the murky-brown, horse-manure-stinking water, and then he looked to Lax. "There's only one way we're getting across this moat today, isn't there?"

Lax looked to the brown water too. "Mmm," he said.

Bert glanced about himself, looked over to the wall that stood before them, that kept them in shadow from the shining midday sun. He gave a long, drawn-out sigh, and then he set about fishing through his knapsack for those cheese and ham sandwiches.

They might as well eat them now before they got totally soaked.

THE GNOMISH COUNCIL OF THE DWINNS

THOROUGHLY SOAKED and reeking of horse manure, Bert scrabbled his way up the town wall which, as it turned out, had a fairly nice array of footholds and grips to ease his way upwards. They'd ended up climbing the wall because Lax had claimed the guards wouldn't open the gates to people who *swam* across the moat. And, if their current stench was anything to go by, Bert had to admit that it was a fairly sensible policy.

As Bert scaled the wall, he reflected that a lifetime down his mine had given him better-than-average climbing abilities since it was now *he* that left Lax trailing in his dust.

Lax glanced up at him, each time further behind, and Bert saw how he was tracing each of his movements to see just how he'd managed to clamber up the wall so quickly.

The trick to it, or so Bert found, was just to keep moving. Hand over hand, foot over foot. Don't look down. That was the key.

A couple of times he found a dizzying spell of vertigo strike him, but he held on tight, feeling his muscles reliable, and his grip never really likely to fail him.

As Bert clambered his way upwards, the kafuffle from the town grew louder and louder. As he got within a head and shoulders of the top of the wall, he identified the noises to himself: a horse's whinny, the *clickety-clack* of a cart bobbing in and out of cobblestones, and, of course, the cackle of a vendor at a marketplace, rounding gnomes up to come buy.

Bert waited patiently for Lax to sidle up alongside him, and then, together, the two of them peered out over the wall and into the town.

For Bert, who had never strayed much further than his local village that rested at the foot of his hill, seeing the amount of gnomes all out in the street at the same time was something of a shock.

There were gnomes of all shapes and sizes, of all different skin tones and dress styles.

His eyeballs near enough rolled right out of their sockets.

He would find his eyes straying over one member of the crowd: a gnome wearing a shirt and tie, for example, and carrying a briefcase, one of those gnomes he was *certain* was not from this Domain.

Another he picked out was a gnome with hair all matted-up in plaits. When he leaned into Lax and requested an explanation, Lax told him that these were known as 'dreadlocks,' though Bert couldn't really make head or tail of them.

Couldn't really see what they were *for*.

Another one, a gnome maybe about twenty, or so, years old,

certainly half the age of Lax, strolled about wearing shorts and sandals and licking at a vanilla ice cream cone.

Music blared through the air: strings, and accordions, and out-of-tune pianos.

There was a whole feeling of frenzy crackling about the place. The way that gnomes in the crowd had to duck and weave to avoid one another on the pavements.

And, of course, the stink of horse manure was now totally overwhelming.

Bert looked to Lax as if asking him what they should do next . . . but he was almost too late considering that Lax was already clambering over the top of the wall, already straddling the top level of bricks. He held on for a moment and then dropped down on the other side with a *crunch* as his shoes made contact with the dirt ground.

Bert hesitated a moment. Unable to quite take all this in. This place, this *town*, was just far more gnomes than he had ever seen in his entire life.

And all at the same time.

He had this strange dual feeling: this buzz of excitement, but also feeling overwhelmed. He felt almost like he wanted to drop back down the other side of the wall, swim his way back across that horse-manure-stinking moat and head off back home . . . but he knew that that simply wasn't an option any longer.

He had spent his entire life obsessing about how the Dwinns was run, and now was his chance to actually meet, face to face, those who ran the administration, to give them a true piece of his mind.

Didn't he deserve at least that much from all the years he'd diligently paid his taxes?

All those years he'd sweated down his mine to send money here, to Cormersbarn.

And now he was determined that he would find out just what had happened to the money, and where it had been spent.

Because, looking about Cormersbarn, he got a good idea of where it had gone.

There were lots of gnomes to maintain in the town, sure, but what about the rest of the funds? The Council must've been sitting on an absolute fortune.

And doing absolutely nothing with it.

Bert took a deep, deep breath, feeling the warm tingle of the horse manure smell burrowing into his lungs, and then, closing his eyes, he tossed himself off the wall and down into the dust.

KING OF THE GHOST TOWN

ARDULL THREW HIMSELF DOWN on the plush, leather sofa in what he assumed had once been the house that'd belonged to the mayor of the village. It was a pleasant red-brick house with a slate roof. Nothing all that fancy on the outside, aside from the tidily kept garden, and the ornamental cherubs.

It all smelled lightly of basil and various other herbs that he'd seen growing out back, in the kitchen garden. Since his stock of yaltas leaves had run out during the offensive on the town, he had tried out chewing various plants that he'd discovered in the kitchen garden.

None of them had given him the same effect the yaltas had, and he'd soon given up on the idea completely.

Outside, he could hear the light dribble of conversation between his troops as they patrolled the town.

This had been such a peaceful Arrive and Occupy.

His gnomes had worked quickly and efficiently, they had shown respect for the town even though the place was empty and for the looting.

But that wasn't the class of gnome they were.

They were better than that.

All of them were professional soldiers, and they acted that way.

He glanced about the walls to the various oil paintings of the gnome he assumed to be the mayor of the town, and his children, and his wife.

They all wore smiles and were looking off into the middle distance with slightly glazed-over stares.

This was the first time that Ardull had actually sat face to face with any sort of impression of the enemy, and he had to admit that they looked a little light-headed.

They all wore that same away-with-the-fairies expression.

The one that, no doubt, the Juttilian spies had seen and decided that they could quite easily take advantage of.

But Ardull had to give them some credit—the Dwindians certainly knew how to clear out in a hurry.

There was no trace of any of the gnomes from before.

He wondered where they'd got to.

And that was what started him off down the path of wondering whether they might be planning some sort of a counterstroke.

Perhaps they were waiting off in the bushes that surrounded the town, all of them armed to their teeth, just waiting for Ardull and his soldiers to file in here before dispensing of them.

. . . But no, Ardull knew he was just being paranoid.

He had soldiers posted all about the town.

Controlling all the entries and exits to the place.

Securing the periphery.

. . . Why *had* he got all paranoid there? There had been no reason to it. That wasn't the sort of gnome he was.

Ardull had got up to his rank because of his clear thinking and almost precisely *because* of his lack of paranoia.

Then again . . . thinking about it for a moment . . . the leaves?

Had that been the source of that paranoid little outburst?

Were they having an ill effect on him?

Some kind of side-effect?

Well, not half an hour ago he'd sent off a crack team to go and retrieve more leaves. Since he'd only sent off a light group, he expected them back before dusk of the next day. Ardull had no plans on moving on from the village until then.

It was best to allow his gnomes to rest a while.

He would allow them to take shelter in the occupied village's homes, though he would insist that they'd treat those houses with great respect.

Because, after all, it could be that some of them would never return back to Juttle, that they might decide to stay here and set up home.

Speaking for himself, Ardull could certainly see himself spending some more time in the Dwinns, the climate really was so pleasant, and the villages genuinely quite quaint.

And as for his poetry, well had it ever gone so wonderfully?

It was like the greens of the place when it was all lit up in the sunshine, well it was nothing short of inspiring.

He would have loved to simply stop right where he was, right now, and spend his days writing his poetry.

But, alas, he still had to carry on with his duty.

With the work that he had been signed up to do.

He needed to lead his gnomes on their Arrive-and-Occupy campaign until they had crippled the centre of power within the Dwinns.

The administrative capital of Cormersbarn.

Take over the Council there.

Then he would be finished. Then he could hang up his uniform, take his retirement, and send for his wife. She could bring his *Grand Compendium of Poetical Musings*, and he could really put some work into pulling the volume all together.

Making it truly his life's work.

Because there was nothing permanent or awe-inspiring through the generations related with blood and murder . . . or, at least, *he* didn't think so.

No, he would much rather see his name go down in the history of Gnomelandia as a grand, haunted soul than as a mighty, unstoppable conqueror and killer.

And, he had to admit to himself, he quite feared that latter title.

Felt the need to rub it out somehow, and stamp his own legacy.

MEANWHILE IN CORMERSBARN

BERT COULD HARDLY take a step without bumping into someone. He had long ago got used to the feel of body warmth, all compounded into one great bloated mass: all sweaty and warm, and impossible to avoid. It was like a wave, in a way, a magnetic wave that simply swept him along on its currents.

The sun heated up the cobblestones and created a kind of furnace on all sides.

He followed on behind Lax, who apparently knew the way to where the Council held office. He made a point never to allow those silver-grey overalls out of his sight, though a couple of times he failed to keep up, and had to jog till he caught up with Lax again.

He could smell roasting nuts, and frying corn, and cooking oil puffed up in clouds, thickening in the air, and making his stomach grumble something awful.

It was his own fault, of course, his hunger.

After all, he'd been the one who'd claimed he was so deter-mined to see the Council that, quite simply, no diversion was to be allowed along the way.

And Lax had taken him seriously.

Bless him.

Still, those sandwiches should've seen him through a little longer. . .

Once Bert had got down at ground level in the town, he'd had that all-too familiar urge to plump a block of fudge onto his tongue. And to chew it down to calm himself.

But he hadn't taken any fudge because he hadn't wanted to lose any of the sensory details that this town held in store, and which it plumped over his nostrils and mouth.

He wanted to drink it all in.

He wanted stories to tell his grandchildren . . . or, well, he'd need to have *children* first if that was to be his goal.

The further that he wove into the crowd, the less he felt like an individual, and the more he felt like he was just part of one great big organism.

A single gnome winding on through this sprawling city.

Finally, Lax turned off the main street and into a side alley.

Though Bert was relishing the experience of the town, he was glad that they were getting off the well-beaten path just for a moment or two.

The experience was just so overwhelming.

So many new sounds and colours, and smells and, he hoped later, tastes.

But that *would* come later, because he had to realise his

previous mission, the reason that he'd come here in the first place to Cormersbarn.

Lax turned back to him when they hit the shade of the side alley, away from the stark sunlight just for a little while, and into a touch of respite. "This is a quick way around—a way we can miss out on all the crowds."

Bert felt like he could breathe easy again, though he had to admit that the horse manure was still extremely thick in the air, and that it would be impossible to escape during their entire stay in the town.

He managed a nod, realising that he actually felt a touch queasy.

He guessed that this was all just too much in some ways.

Lax led him on down another series of winding alleys, past market stalls that sold all sorts of oddities: skulls, and candles, and strange-coloured liquids in vials.

Though Bert would've liked to ask a few questions about them, firstly he didn't feel quite well, and secondly he guessed that Lax probably knew as little about the objects as he did.

That old saying about 'in the kingdom of the blind, the one-eyed gnome is king' came to mind.

And Lax was that one-eyed gnome right now.

Lax brought them before a staircase which led upwards from the side alley, and out along a ledge, and back over the main street, still sprawling with bustling gnomes.

They headed on along the creaking wooden planks, leaving the crowds below them behind, and then crossed over to the other side.

Another couple of twists of alley later and Bert found himself facing off with the central square of Cormersbarn, and their destination:

The Seat of the Council.

THERE, AT LAST?

BERT DRANK IN the sight with his eyes. He'd seen the place in photographs, of course, ones that he'd seen on the market back home, from the travellers who'd wandered through the village. But seeing it for the first time, with his own two eyes, meant those photographs were really no comparison at all.

Light-yellow tiles were laid on the ground of the main square, all of them reflecting the beaming sunlight. The fountain in the centre featured a gnome family: a gentleman gnome, a lady-wife gnome, and a child gnome, all of them grinning away, their features chiselled out of stone.

Though Bert had never been much of a great chiseller himself, he *could* appreciate great work when he saw it. And this sculpture, of the gnome family, was among the best pieces he'd ever seen . . . and though he'd seen it in photographs before, now it just seemed totally new to him for the first time.

Here, in the main square of Cormersbarn, there were hardly

any gnomes. None of the bustling crowds, none of the vendors with their stalls. Only a handful of gnomes who looked to Bert like tourists. That was to say that they had cameras hanging down from their necks and were snapping photos of one another at just about every opportunity.

Off at the corners of the square, and about the periphery, he saw that guards with flat caps pressed down over their hair, well-combed beards and stern expressions marked onto their faces, stood about.

He also noticed that none of the guards seemed to be armed at all, so he wondered just what use they were, other than ornamental.

And if there was one thing a gnome hated above all else it was to be *ornamental*.

But Bert was skipping over by far the biggest feature of the square without so much as batting an eyelid.

There was just so much for him to take in.

Now he turned his attention to it.

Bert eyed the Seat of the Council up ahead—nothing less than a fully-fledged palace, blocky and slightly intimidating, though he expected that he'd be just a little more intimidated if he didn't know that a real bunch of softies ran the place, or that he most likely paid for a significant portion of that fine brick-work with his hard-earned taxes.

The building itself was a light-pink colour: probably what some gnomes would term 'salmon' if they had time to do so while they robbed your pockets.

A light scent of cinnamon seemed to eek out about the square, and Bert sucked that in, just as he had sucked in every smell about the town since he'd arrived here . . . he couldn't miss so much as a single odour.

Lax guided him along, over the main square, and then they headed up the steps of the Seat, and up to the main doors where a pair of equally stern-faced, and equally *unarmed*, guards awaited them.

Neither of the guards would look them in the eye. They just kept their heads tilted back, staring not quite at the sky, but not quite at the rooftops beyond that either.

"Uh," Bert said, starting somewhat unconvincingly, "we've come to see the Council."

The guards didn't even look when Bert addressed them directly, continuing to stare off into space. One of them *did* reply, however. "Permission?"

". . . What?" Bert said.

"Permission," the guard said, this time not a question but a demand.

Bert glanced back at Lax, and his flame-red hair.

Lax gave him a shrug in return.

Bert turned back to the guard. "Look," he said, "I'm a citizen of Earknork and I was wondering if I might be able to go in and meet with the Council." He paused for a moment and then added, "If they're not too busy."

The guard made a pout from his lips, but still didn't look over at them. "You must get permission to meet with the Council—you think that they have time to speak to every gnome who comes wandering through here?"

Bert decided to go a little more direct. "We've . . . *I've* come a long way, see? All the way from Earknork, and, well, I was just hoping that they might . . ."

The guard let out an enormous sigh, and then jerked his thumb over his shoulder, to the side of the building.

Bert followed his thumbnail and saw the queue snaking around the corner.

Several gnomes all queued up.

"Go and get in line with the rest of them," the guard said. "Come back here when you've got your permission."

Bert looked to Lax, back to the guard, nodded and gave him an almost muted, "Thanks," before he stole off to join the queue.

Just as he and Lax turned the corner, he heard the guard call out after him.

"And you might think about taking a shower too!"

A GOOD OLD QUEUE

I F THERE was one thing that had Bert like the proverbial
fish right out of water it was this concept of queuing.
Having lived in a village of less than a hundred population his
whole life, and never having ventured out of the place for more
than a daytrip, Bert had never *ever* had the need to join a queue.

But here he found that he was going head on with a whole
bunch of firsts.

The queue seemed to consist of a few hundred gnomes.

Certainly more gnomes than there were in Bert's village.

And everyone wore an impatient expression that told Bert
they'd been waiting in line for an awfully long time.

Lax stood at Bert's elbow, and stood on his tiptoes, apparently trying to see over the crowd, as if there might be some sort
of a shortcut that they could take right to the front of the line.

It was strange, Bert had lived his life as if he was special—as
if he was a one-off individual, but being here, having arrived to

the capital, he saw that he was very far from being an individual, he was simply one of many citizens, no better or worse than his neighbour in this queue.

. . . Though very likely better off.

The queue moved along at the *shuffle* of feet along the pale-yellow tiled floor, and Bert could certainly see no sort of an end in sight . . . though, to be honest, he really had no idea what to expect at the end of a line anyway.

He looked to Lax, as if he might have some sort of a better idea of what they might do—how they might actually get in to see the Council in either of their lifetimes.

But Lax looked like he was all cleaned out.

To be fair to him, he *had* brought Bert here, to Cormersbarn, and he'd made a noble attempt to get them over the moat too.

Bert decided that now it was his turn to show just a little initiative.

And so, he went with the tactic that had always worked for him back home—the tactic that never failed to get him results.

He dipped his hand into his trouser pocket and produced a wad of notes.

His billfold.

The effect of it was almost instantaneous. It was like just the paper money he carried made a supersonic sound that only gnomes could hear . . . or a note that only *Dwindians* could hear, anyway . . .

The up-thrust of him bringing out his billfold was that everyone standing ahead of them in the queue looked over their shoulders.

Grandmothers with candyfloss hair, mothers with blouses buttoned up to the saggy skin of their throats, fathers wearing waistcoats and who had sharp eyes that seemed to constantly skitter about in that way Bert had learned to recognise as a Dwindian looking to turn a fast profit, by hook or by crook.

Bert even noticed a little girl, surely no older than ten or eleven years old, still sucking on a dummy, stop bawling out her eyes at her parents for whatever it was that she wanted, and look right over at him, eyes wide and lips slightly parted in wonder.

Oh yes, Bert was the money all right.

And he knew it.

So, with Lax at his elbow, keeping him close to him, he skirted about the queue, fobbing each gnome off with a crisp note of their own.

In a way it warmed his heart to see the way that they all smiled at him, how there was a certain glimmer in their eyes as they accepted his money . . . his *bribe*.

A few of them even gave up queuing all together and Bert surmised that, most likely, they'd only joined the queue in the first place, wanted to go see the Council, so that they might have a chance of pocketing some loose change.

Just another refresher that he could *never ever* trust a Dwindian gnome.

Scammers, the lot of them.

Before too long . . . in less than five minutes, in fact . . . he found himself and Lax standing at the front of the queue. A velvet rope draped down across the side entrance to the building, and Bert could see a red carpet leading into the inside of the place.

He guessed that the councillors all had quite a high opinion of themselves.

Or did it say that they had a high opinion of the gnomes who came here to petition them?

He really couldn't decide.

A prim woman with lightly-coifed hair and finely-painted crimson lips stood at the rope. She carried a clipboard and had black eyes, those ones that made Bert think about his good old mine, now neglected for a couple of days and a night.

She was dressed in a blue-grey trouser suit, and wore a light pink blouse underneath, peeping through the lapels of her jacket. She pursed her lips in a pout and looked both Bert and Lax over, wincing slightly at their no doubt putrid smell.

Maybe that guard had been onto something when he'd suggested that he and Lax go and catch themselves a shower.

The other Dwindians in the queue hadn't complained about the sodden, stinking money, though . . .

No time for a shower now, anyway, and not really enough money to hand out to a fresh queue of gnomes later on.

Getting to the front of the queue had actually turned out to be quite expensive.

"This way," she said, and then, with a neat turn of heel, unclipped the crimson rope and allowed both Bert and Lax inside.

ON THE MOVE AGAIN

ARDULL LOOKED OVER his troops as they filed on out through the village, catching up with him at his side, moving on up the hill like a ragged snake.

He looked down over the village that they had conquered without so much as setting eyes on the enemy, and he felt his heart well in his throat to think that he had to leave the place because, and he only knew it now, standing here, that he had fallen in love with the mayor's house, with that plush, leather sofa, the red-bricks, the kitchen garden there.

But there was at least consolation that he could calm himself with, and that was that the yaltas leaves, a fresh batch of them, for his personal use solely, had arrived early that morning.

And Ardull was making very good use of them, indeed.

Why, standing up here, on this faintly overcast day, the smell of rain in the air, he was chomping quite contentedly on the yaltas leaves, feeling his saliva thicken with each one of his bites. The way he estimated it, he would have leaves enough to see him through a solid few weeks, and they'd keep him going on.

With that same heaviness in his heart, and with no opportunity to withdraw his notebook and try to get some sort of order to these feelings in the form of verse, he turned his back on that quiet little village—the village that had had no name that he could discern.

Oh, there had been a signpost with a name scrawled on it in Dwindish, but it was nothing that he could decipher. And he hadn't been able to round up a translator anywhere . . . anybody who was half competent in Dwindish he had sent on ahead to work as spies in Cormersbarn, and he planned to rendezvous with them when he brought his troop a little closer to the capital.

Jeorge had made a go of translating the sign, but it had just come out as a jumbled phrase that Ardull couldn't make head nor tail of.

But this, really, was immaterial, a mere trifle, because when they got closer to the city, he would need his spies, because if there was to be any sort of opposition, it would happen right there, in the capital of the Dwinns, and it was Ardull's duty to ensure that no more blood was shed than was necessary . . . not of Dwindians *or* of Juttilians.

That was his goal.

Once he had all his gnomes assembled, leaving behind only a light garrison in the town, he led their march forwards, away from the village, his heart seeming to grow heavier still.

But he pushed them on.

Not allowing the group to stop off until it was well into the evening, with dusk riding on their heels, and the moon already high up in the sky.

By his calculations, from what he'd seen from the maps, they could easily be on the outskirts of Cormersbarn by tomorrow afternoon, and so he called Jeorge into his tent, once he'd got himself set up for the night, and he had him arrange for the spies waiting for them in Cormersbarn to be made aware of what was going on.

Jeorge looked a little pudgier than usual, and Ardull put this down to them having been parked in that village for a long while.

There *was* an awfully tasty little bakery with whole assort-ments of cupcakes, and donuts, and other sugary sweets all left behind by the fled citizens.

Why, even Ardull himself had noticed that he had developed something of a saggy little gut.

It was incredible how much weight one could put on in so few hours.

Jeorge was doing his blinking thing—that nervous twitch thing he did whenever he had some bad news to deliver . . . or what Jeorge interpreted as being bad news.

"Sir?" he said.

"Yes," Ardull said, lying back on his bunk and already dreading whatever it was Jeorge was about to tell him.

That was the thing about his assistant, the way that often the problems he outlined were completely surmountable—easily solved—but it was just the manner he laid them out. As if he was informing Ardull of a soon-to-arrive apocalypse.

"There's a, uh, *slight* problem with our plan, sir. You know, sir, our plan to march to the edge of Cormersbarn, and for us, to, uh, set up camp there in preparation for a strike early the next morning?"

Probably among the top five of Jeorge's most annoying habits had to be that way that he regurgitated well-discussed plans . . . it might even have been vying for the number-one spot. Ardull barely suppressed a sigh and reiterated to himself the important of patience, if not for a general then for a poetical soul. "What *is* it?" he said, not quite able to keep his frustrations completely out of that 'is.'

"Uh, uh, uh," Jeorge said, sounding like a blathering loon.

"Go on!"

Jeorge gave Ardull a flicker of a smile, met Ardull's gaze for a sliver of a second, and then seemed to get all interested in the fabric of the tent. "It's the, uh, the *moat*, sir."

"The moat?"

"Yes," Jeorge said, "the moat that flows about the town, it's, uh, it's been flooded over the past few days, sir."

"Flooded?"

"Yes, and it's, uh, covered up the bridges, sir."

Ardull screwed up his forehead, trying to make some sort of sense of this. "So, what you're saying is that the water of the moat is too high to use the bridges?"

"Yes, sir, that's exactly it."

Perhaps Jeorge was lucky that there wasn't a blunt object nearby to get thrown at him, though, thinking about it later on, Ardull realised he'd had his poetical notebook the whole while . . . but even if he'd known he probably wouldn't have thrown it.

Ardull brought Jeorge into focus, and wondered whether he might be better off picking out a less annoying personal assistant from his wide array of abiding soldiers.

Patience.

He *had* to remember patience.

He fixed Jorge in his gaze, this time there would be no getting away for him, and then he said, "Well, if the moat's flooded then I suppose we'll have to swim across."

Jorge looked a touch doubtful. "But, sir, from the intelligence I've received all the reports indicate that . . . that, well . . ."

"Yes?" Ardull said, his temper being truly tested now, and his poetical writing time being unceremoniously cut into.

"The thing's practically *sewage*, sir."

"So?"

Jeorge's eyes seemed to bulge from their sockets. His complexion turned a deep mauve colour, and Ardull thought, just for a moment, that he might have to call a medic into his tent.

But Jeorge pulled it together, together enough for him to smile vaguely, to nod, and then to hot tail it out of Ardull's tent.

Ardull let loose that long-held sigh, and then he folded his hands back behind his head and stared up at the weave of his tent roof.

Really, sometimes it was impossible to get good help.

Some gnomes seemed to see problems just about *everywhere*.

RED TAPE

BERT COULD FEEL that familiar smell of marble wafting back at him, that smell that reminded him of his mansion, of his home. At least the councillors had some shred of taste about them. He thought of plucking a piece of fudge out and lying it down on his tongue, but decided against it, not knowing just how ceremonial this thing was . . . and how smart he was supposed to present himself.

The air was cool, and he felt his skin breaking out in pimples. He could hear his footsteps, those of the lady who led them along the narrow passageway, and Lax's echoing all about them.

Though he would never have admitted so much aloud, he could feel his heart pounding with his excitement. The blood rushing up to his head.

He was a little anxious about this.

Despite knowing well how he had a right to be here.

They turned a corner, entering into a passageway in total

darkness, and, just like that, the woman turned on them, eyes just about visible, and moving swiftly between the two of them. "The meeting you are about to have is to determine whether the matter you seek to raise with the Council can be easily dealt with by an auxiliary, and whatever action, if action is needed to be taken, needs the Council's intervention." She clasped her lips shut, squeezing all the blood out of them, and then added, with an arched eyebrow, "Is that clear?"

Bert could only allow himself to nod in reply.

The woman sniffed a couple of times, then said, "Have you two just crawled through a latrine or something?"

Bert swallowed hard, and then said, "Yes, something like that."

She rolled her eyes and led them on along the corridor, and up to a pair of thick oak doors with various decorative engravings all embedded about the edge.

This, too, reminded Bert of some work he'd had done to his front doors a few years back.

She cast a glare back over them, raised her eyebrows, and then swung the twin doors open for them, revealing a lightly gleaming candlelit interior.

A warm glow seemed to emanate from the place, and Bert could feel that warmth bringing out a bit of colour from his cheeks. And could feel the slight prickle of fresh sweat leaking out from him.

Only now did he wonder whether he should've got himself and Lax set up with a hotel . . . and a sturdy en suite, before they'd ventured on out to speak with the Council.

Ah, well, too late now.

With smart *clacks* of her heels, the woman led them into the room.

It resembled the Grand Library back home, the way that there were leathered volumes stuffed into all the varnished mahogany bookshelves. And the glossy wooden floors too. And the proud desk which stood up with rigid iron legs.

An even more rigid, waist-coated figure sat behind the desk, currently scrawling away on some piece of parchment. He had white hair, where he had hair at all, and wore a pair of gilt-framed glasses. The nib of his quill made a sharp *scratch* on the parchment.

A fireplace roared behind him, flames leaping up the chimney and blowing away the gloom in the room. When Bert looked about him, he realised that all the windows were boarded up, as if this gnome was allergic to daylight or something.

Thinking about it, Bert guessed that they really weren't that different. Bert spent almost his entire life, almost all daylight, down his mine chomping on rock, searching for valuable minerals and such.

This man, well, Bert thought that he'd find out what he did pretty soon.

"Master Yorn?" the woman said, in a quieter, much softer voice.

A voice that Bert could tell she reserved for speaking with her employers, or those that she respected.

Given how she'd spoken to them before, Bert supposed that she didn't consider either him or Lax one of those things.

The white-haired gnome said, "Hmm?" but continued his scratching on the parchment, not looking up from his work.

"Some more who'd like permission."

The white-haired gnome, Master Yorn, gave an arthritic nod, and continued to scrawl across his parchment.

The woman gave Bert and Lax a final-warning glare, and then she clacked on out of the room, apparently to go off and see to her queue, to check that nothing was getting out of order . . . if there was any queue at all left now that Bert had bribed most of them away.

She brought the doors shut behind her as she went, and the air temperature seemed to rise. The sweat began to trickle down Bert's back as they stood there before, the apparently very busy, Master Yorn.

JUST A LITTLE LONGER

F OR THE NEXT FIVE MINUTES, Master Yorn
continued to scrawl away, and Bert found himself lost in
those rhythmic scratches, got to imagining that someone was
scratching away at the inside of his skull.

Finally, Master Yorn leaned back in his chair, eyed Bert and
Lax over the tops of his glasses, said, "Just a minute," and rested
his quill down on his desk and went about folding up the parchment he'd been writing on.

After it seemed like he'd folded the parchment a solid dozen
times, and then placed it into an envelope, licked it, then sealed
it, he put the closed envelope down on the desk beside him, on
top of a whole pile of envelopes, apparently to be sent off.

Bert wondered if this was the gnome who'd written him out
those hundreds of form responses as he'd turned in his tax
returns every year.

"Yes?" Master Yorn said, pressing his fingertips together and looking over the arch he created.

Bert exchanged glances with Lax, and then turned back to Master Yorn. "We've come here today to seek permission . . ."

Master Yorn sniffed the air and then made a wrinkled-up face. His voice sounded almost dusty when he spoke, as if someone only had to blow some air in his general direction to knock him off his feet. "Can you smell that?" he said.

Bert kept his eyes fixed on Master Yorn. "Perhaps it's just something unpleasant burning in one of the logs on the fireplace."

Master Yorn tilted his head to one side, considering this, and then he said, "Hmm," apparently accepting Bert's explanation.

Bert was glad.

"Right," Bert said, "you might know my name, I've been *quite* lucrative over the years for your taxing operation, and I have also held quite a weighty correspondence with the Council." He paused for effect, and then said, "I am Flaughterbert Mhyresgnome."

It was like the room soaked up Bert's name, but, at the same time, he was certain that Master Yorn had heard him just fine.

Still, he felt the need to repeat himself.

"Flaughterbert Mhyresgnome," he said again, a little quieter this time.

Master Yorn just blinked in the gloomy room, looking to Bert a little like a startled mole the way that he parted his lips.

"You, uh," Bert said, shooting sidelong glance at Lax, "you haven't, or, uh, don't . . ."

Master Yorn blinked a couple more times and then he peered upwards at the ceiling, mouthing, apparently, Bert's full name.

And then, all of a sudden, without warning, he thrust an index finger into the air, and said, "Yes, yes, yes! I think I *have* heard of you, Flaughterbert, yes, I can recall your letters."

Bert felt the tightness in his chest loosen just a little, and he allowed himself to breathe out.

Master Yorn helped himself up with the arms of his chair. And trudged over to the bookshelf behind him, and he ran that same index finger he'd used to signal his breakthrough along the spines of the volumes there.

Finally, after what seemed like hours of searching, he tugged one of the volumes off the shelf, and somehow, tottering about beneath its weight, brought it over to his desk and set it down there.

When it landed, it made a heavy *thud*, and dust puffed up.

Master Yorn screwed up his eyes and blew the dust away, and then, with a brief glance over at Bert and Lax, he turned his attention downwards.

He flipped the well-thumbed, yellowed pages swiftly as he searched through the book, looking for some specific entry, before, again without warning, he let loose a triumphant, and slightly croaky, "Ah-*ha!*" coupled with, what was becoming, the trademark index finger thrusting upwards into the air.

He looked over to Lax and Bert, apparently inviting them silently over to have a look at just what he'd uncovered there in the volume.

Bert broke out of his daze and, with Lax alongside, he sidled up to the desk and looked over the volume. There, pasted onto the page, he recognised his scrawled handwriting. When he checked the date he'd written at the top in the flicker from the firelight, he saw that this must've been the first letter he'd sent to the Council.

A glint in his eye, Master Yorn looked to Bert. "Yes, Flaughterbert, I do remember you. All these letters, all these years."

Bert decided that now was the time to press home his point, the whole reason that he'd left his incredibly comfortable mansion in the hills behind. "And did you ever pass on any of these letters to the Council?"

Master Yorn held his gaze, his lips curled slightly at the edges in a wry smile and then he said, with a new-found vigour in his voice, "Oh, heavens no!"

ACTUALLY REALLY QUITE ANNOYING

"WHAT?" Bert said. "I mean"—he fixed Master Yorn with his glance, half watching as he peeled back yet more pages of that volume to uncover letters from Bert, year upon year, him dishing out suggestions for the Council—"you never, uh, *never* passed anything along?"

Master Yorn continued turning pages and shook his head as he did so. "No point to it—the Council aren't interested in hearing from every crackpot who sends in a letter."

Bert felt a sharp jab at the base of his gut at being called a 'crackpot' but then, thinking about it a little harder, thinking about the stereotypical image of letter writers he'd built up over his years of thinking, he guessed that there was no real reason why he shouldn't fall into that bracket.

Better to leave it for now, anyway.

Better just to get on with things.

Bert fixed Master Yorn in his gaze, seeing that he kept

turning the pages, uncovering letter after letter signed, Flaugh-terbert Mhyresgnome.

To think of all the time he'd wasted with those letters, scrib-bling away, thinking about them getting received at the Council and given thorough consideration, when, all along, they'd simply ended up here in this dead-letter office.

Master Yorn was giving a dry sort of chuckle as he continued to turn the pages, and Bert found himself feeling increasingly ill towards the old man.

"Look," Bert said, "we've come here, to Cormersbarn so that we can have an audience with the Council, I have some suggestions that I believe they might be interested in."

Master Yorn nodded away, but it was clear that he was still totally occupied with the volume lying on the desk before him.

If Bert wasn't mistaken, he was sure that he could see the shimmer of tears of laughter fogging up the man's eyes . . . well, at least he'd given the gnome some good years of entertainment if nothing else.

Master Yorn continued to nod away, but still Bert wasn't sure he'd heard. This was confirmed when Master Yorn thrust that index finger of his up in the air again and said, with a face-split-ting smile, "Listen to this one, this one is just *wonderful!*"

Bert looked to Lax who, he was a little annoyed to see, was looking on goggle-eyed, and apparently anxious to hear what the fuss was about.

"'Dear Council,'" Master Yorn began, "'Within please find my yearly tax rates all paid and correct, and I hope that they find you all well.

"'It is with a slightly heavy heart that I look out upon my town, the town of Earknork, as I'm sure you are well aware of from our previous correspondence, and see no sort of inter-village transport infrastructure—nothing so much as a horse-and-cart service, or anything of the like.

"I have noted, throughout my studies of the Dwinns that gnomes across the breadth of the Domain prefer not to commit to using horses, instead opting to go by foot to wherever they need to go.

"And it is the conclusion of my studies that I must point out that this is more likely to be due to a lack of any organised inter-village system rather than a lack of ingenuity on the gnomes' part . . . and I should also point out that I, myself, have such little interest in travel because of this rather *odd* restriction that plagues our lands.

"And so, I put it to you, oh noble councilmen"—Bert winced just a little at that one, at how, back when he'd been a fresh-faced millionaire he'd nurtured such a grand respect for the Council—"that you should consider such a system when thinking through the implementation of this year's taxation, because I believe that it would revolutionise the way that all of the Dwinns functions.

"I shall, as ever, be available for consultation by post (as I have neither the service or the time to reach Cormersbarn by foot).

"Yours sincerely, Flaughterbert Mhyresgnome.'"

Master Yorn managed to stay straight-faced for a couple of moments before the uneasy veneer cracked completely and he gave a couple of aged chortles.

"Well," Bert said, feeling just a touch slighted by this display, "it was just an idea, and it seemed to me, back home, that it was something that the Council was somewhat short of. Just an idea for the Dwinns to catch up with the rest of Gnomelandia, you know."

He eyed Lax as if he might find some sort of support from him, though he knew that the blacksmith most likely didn't think much outside of his own village.

Bert continued, "From what I hear there are some Domains of the world that now have devices that make it simple to speak to someone at the other end of the Domain, by using a kind of speaking tube, you see it func—"

"Yes," Master Yorn said, still smiling, "they call it a telephone."

Bert felt a shock skitter up his spine. He hadn't expected the old gnome to know something like that. "Yes," Bert said, "that was the name of it."

Master Yorn just nodded along now, gently closing up the volume, stalking his way back to the shelf where he'd slid it off. As he worked to jam it back into its place, he spoke over his shoulder. "You have much to learn about how things work here, in the Dwinns, Flaughterbert. You assume that things are the way they are because it's all laid out, because it's all planned out so poorly."

Bert couldn't quite understand what Master Yorn was getting at, but he thought it better not to break his flow with questions . . . not till he'd filled him in on this.

"What you will learn, when you meet with the Council, what you will *begin* to understand about the Dwinns is that all of this"—Master Yorn swept his arms about himself to indicate the entire library—"it's all here for a reason."

Bert slipped Lax a sidelong glance. He knew this route quite well, it was often employed by those same scammers who came knocking on the door of his mansion for their shammy charities. This one, he could tell, was headed down a religious route . . . imploring him to donate to placate this or that god.

But he held still and waited out the silence broken only by the crackling logs of the fireplace. Then, when it was clear that Master Yorn wasn't going to say anything more, he spoke up.

"So, you're going to give us permission to speak with the Council?"

Master Yorn gave him a hardy smile, then nodded his head. "Yes," he said, "you shall meet with them tomorrow morning."

Finally.

Bert could almost feel his heart doing a little jig, but he kept himself under control long enough to take the piece of parchment that Master Yorn scrawled out their permission on.

He thanked Master Yorn and then, with Lax at his side, headed on out to go and find somewhere to bed down for the night.

Somewhere he could get a hot shower.

MUCH CLOSER NOW

ARDULL LAY BACK on his field bunk and stared up at the ceiling, his notebook with his latest entries of the poem he was working on, sprawled on his chest, its pages all fluttering outwards like feathers.

Once again, for maybe the third time that hour, he reached out across to his bag of yaltas leaves, took a good pinch of them between finger and thumb, then deposited them on the tip of his tongue.

He chewed and chewed, growing more feverish as he did so.

That warming feeling returned to his jaw, and all his worries, all the aches and pains in his muscles, seemed to fade away at once.

He had come to the realisation that he didn't really feel normal—*properly* normal—without a good old bunch of yaltas leaves in his mouth.

It was actually quite concerning.

And he was beginning to worry about himself.

Earlier that day, as they'd trekked on down to the valley where they'd pitched camp, now only a short distance from Cormersbarn, a fight had broken out between a pair of his soldiers.

He'd taken it upon himself to go down there personally and break it up.

And when he had, when he dragged one of the gnomes off the other, brought him up to look him in the eye so that he might receive his dressing down in the proper manner, he'd seen the veins all standing out in his eyes, that half-crazed look.

A look that he'd grown to know quite well since every time he looked in the mirror, after his supply of yaltas had run out, he would see the same.

And he knew it was the look of addiction.

Of not being able to get a fix.

And though he had recognised it right away, he hadn't thought to offer the soldier some leaves from the pouch he kept in the pocket of his jacket, though surely that would've been the best way to let off some of the tension in the fraught encounter.

No, he'd reprimanded the soldiers for fighting, given them punishment, by way of having to clean field latrines, and then he'd set off, on his merry way, to the front of the column.

His own mouth filled with yaltas.

It was his fault, after all, he had been the one responsible for getting the gnomes under his command hooked on the stuff and, he supposed, the responsibility of getting them off it also fell to him.

But that was much easier said than done considering that he now only had enough of a supply to fuel his own habit.

. . . There was no way around it now, no time for him to send gnomes back to those jungles of the Poot a second time for them to snaffle up yet more yaltas. He needed all the gnomes he could get here and now for the assault on Cormersbarn, whether they were coming down off drugs or not.

Ardull was brought around from his deliberations when he heard the chatter outside his tent. And the unmistakable tone of Jeorge's voice.

Yes, it was that time again . . .

Time for him to experience his assistant *again*.

Sure enough, he heard that half *slap*, half *scratch* up against the flap of his tent—that sound that sort of passed for a knock out here in the field—and Ardull called him in.

As Ardull looked Jeorge over, and the pair of gnomes who entered behind him, he realised that he'd clean forgotten about the meeting.

That he was meeting with the spies who'd been planted in Cormersbarn, the ones who'd been in charge of gathering the intelligence they'd need to complete their acquisition of the Dwinns Domain.

Both his spies were several inches shorter than Jeorge, and they both wore fuzzy, blue-and-black striped jumpers. Their beards had grown long and tangled—much longer and more tangled than he would've permitted had they been serving in uniform—and he saw . . . just a glimmer . . . yes, he was sure, one of them had got his ear pierced and now wore a silver stud there that glinted in the light from his gas lamp.

Ardull propped himself up on his bunk and looked them over

with fresh eyes, hoping that he didn't look too doped up from all the yaltas he'd chewed over the course of the day.

One thing was for certain, as soon as this Arrive-and-Occupy offensive was concluded, he'd look into getting himself some professional help for this fledgling drug addiction of his.

"Well?" Ardull said, eyeing his spies.

One of them stepped forwards, the one with the earring.

Ardull met him with a cool eye. "Not you," he said.

The gnome with the earring looked a touch confused but he didn't protest, allowing the other gnome to step forwards and take his place.

Ardull kept up his glare on the gnome with the earring for just a few more moments. He knew the face of a spy who'd been having a little *too much* fun at the expense of the Juttilian Army and he didn't much like it.

He shuddered to think what else he might find out if he pried into their situation a little further . . . a tattoo perhaps?

The gnome without the earring informed him that the moat was still very much flooded, and that crossing over the bridges was totally out of the question.

On the plus side, though, there was next to no defence in the city . . . which was to say that the concept of guards *did* exist but they were unarmed, and, well . . . *ornamental*.

Ardull flinched a touch at *that* word. Though he'd served in the army his whole life he had found it difficult to ever get a grasp of even the basics of the fundamental putty mouth.

The information really changed nothing, though he expressed dry gratitude for what they'd brought him.

He dismissed the spies, fixing the one with the earring with an especially ominous and leering glare, just so he knew where he stood.

He ordered both spies to get themselves suited up for the offensive the next day.

He wasn't taking any chances.

Not when the outcome of the campaign was on the line.

THE BIG DAY

I T WAS FUNNY how much good a long night's sleep and a few dozen showers could do a gnome, or, at least, that was certainly how Bert felt about it.

After he'd got into the hotel room the night before, and he'd thoroughly cleansed himself of watered-down manure: gnomic and equine alike, he'd simply dropped right onto his bed and been out for the count till he'd heard Lax sneaking in around, his gnome sense told him, two or three o'clock in the morning, smelling thickly of fermentation and pipe smoke.

He said nothing, though, made no sound to let Lax know that he was even awake.

Why shouldn't the boy enjoy his time in the big city?

It wasn't like Lax was under Bert's employ or anything, was it?

Right now, standing over Lax's sleeping, snoring body, all suited and booted for the big day, Bert thought about giving Lax a couple of hearty pokes in the ribs, to wake him up for the meeting with the Council but, in the end, he decided against it on two counts.

One was that he didn't feel like waking the boy considering he'd be well short of a night's sleep, and, in any case, Bert knew the city well enough now . . . well enough to get himself to the Seat.

Another was that, well, to be honest, following that *hug* back at Phardoe, and the misunderstanding that had followed, it'd been, all told, quite a good feat of Lax to agree to sharing a twin-bed room with him.

And Bert didn't want to get him thinking otherwise.

If Lax could misinterpret a well-intention hug then there was no telling how he would take a couple of well-aimed fingers to the chest.

So he left him there, sleeping.

Outside, the morning sun beamed down on the still half-asleep streets. As Bert got stuck into his march, he noticed various vendors trudging about, unfolding their multi-coloured marquee tents for the day ahead. He also spotted just a few elderly women sweeping the dust off their front doorsteps, and he took care to pick his way about those clouds of dirt, not wanting to turn up at the Seat looking like he was wearing half a road.

He'd given his beard a good combing this morning, too, got it into that nice fluffy state he'd only managed on the most formal of occasions with shampoo and conditioner, a state that he usually avoided since he normally just gave it a good soaping down.

He almost had the urge to whistle as he took in the light-pink building, as he stepped up to the front doors of the Seat, that same sturdy oak that they'd used in the library doors that Master Yorn had sat behind.

He grasped his envelope containing the permission tight and then handed it over to the waiting guard—the same one from the day before standing there and looking just as unimpressed as he had the day before . . . but at least this time he wasn't wrinkling up his nose too.

The guard worked quickly, slipped his bony finger through the flap of the envelope and then fished out the folded-up parchment inside. He read it fast, his eyes skittering from side to side and then he licked his thumb and rubbed it against the crimson seal that Master Yorn had stamped on there by way of authentication.

Apparently it passed the test.

And the guard gestured for Bert to pass, for him to go in through the oak doors.

Bert didn't wait about either, just casting a quick glance over his shoulder to the glorious sunny day that now shone down on the central square of the town, to those pale-yellow tiles all lit up in its rays.

Inside the front hall of the building, Bert found himself greeted with another pair of guards who made a ceremony of patting him down.

For what, Bert really hadn't a clue given that there were no weapons to be found anywhere in the Dwinns.

And they gave the whole routine up a couple of seconds later, pointing him off along the oak-panelled corridor, hung with dingy oil paintings with lifeless-looking, regal gnomes staring down.

Bert didn't hang around for any further explanation, not wanting to get himself turfed out at this point. And so he skipped on along the thick carpet and onwards to a door which stood right at the end of the corridor.

On the door was a gilded placard which read: The Deliberation Room.

He guessed that this was the place.

Bert gave the fudge he'd shoved between his jaws on waking this morning a farewell crunch and then swallowed it down.

Rules and regulations or no, he knew that he had to put his best foot forwards.

He got a rush from the sugary aftertaste of the fudge, and he could feel it churning about in his gut already, warming him from the inside like a fireplace on a chilly winter's day. He breathed in the polish that seemed to thicken in the air, trying to get himself calmer. Trying to slow his pulse, and keep his heart from ticking on so relentlessly.

On the other side of the door, he could hear mumbling tones.

And he knew that the Deliberation Room was already filled with the councilmen, and women.

He just needed to knock.

He only realised that he was shaking when he brought his hand up, brought his knuckles a few inches from the oak door. He saw that all the colour had drained out of his hand.

He swallowed hard.

Sank his teeth into his bottom lip.

And knocked.

"COME IN"

BERT FELT HIMSELF shuddering all over now. But he held himself together long enough to turn the brass doorknob, to thrust the door inwards, and then to step over the threshold and into the sun-draped room within.

It was warm here, warmer than he would've expected. He guessed that this was one of those rooms which the sun hit from the very earliest hours of the morning.

For a couple of seconds he was blinded by the brightness of the sunlight as it beamed in through the window, seeming to make everything metal in the room glimmer back at him.

In that dizzy second, his forearm raised up to shield his eyes, he speculated whether this might be a cynical effort on the part of the Council, to make whatever old drip had decided to come and speak with them feel innately uncomfortable.

But, as Bert's eyes got better used to the light, he was able to bring his forearm down, and to take in those sat about him, occupying the leather-upholstered chairs, with their rounded backs. Each gnome held their hands clutched on the long, circular walnut desk.

Seven of them in all.

Just looking those hands over, even from the safety of the doorway, Bert could see that not one of them had done, what his father would've called, a hard day's work in their lives.

Either that or they used some industrial-strength hand moisturiser, and he'd very much like to get the name of the brand so he could pick some up on his way back home . . .

"Mister . . . ?"

Bert swivelled about. Followed the female voice that had come at him from the end of the table. When the sunlight cleared just a touch from his eyes, he made out who it was: the woman from the day before, the one who'd been guarding the queue so relentlessly.

Today she wore a light-pink trouser suit which he supposed was meant to coordinate with the colour of the building. Her lips were painted the same shade of pink. Her black eyes peered out at him.

Bert remembered himself. Forced on a smile and then said, "Mhyresgnome. Flaughterbert Mhyresgnome."

The woman scribbled something down on a piece of parchment before her, an eyebrow raised. Then, apparently finished, she glanced up at him, indicated the empty chair which stood opposite her, and was at the head of the table.

Keeping up his nervous smile, Bert took his place in the proffered chair. When he sat, he noticed that the leather was soft and he sank right down into it. He wondered, a little distantly, just what they stuffed the cushion with.

When he turned his attention back to the table, he noticed the corners of the woman's mouth turning up in a vague smile. "I trust that you've had a good wash since yesterday."

Bert blinked a couple of times, considering a witty comeback for just a second. But then, at the last moment, he decided against it. Better for him just to make a good impression on these important ladies and gentlemen. So he just smiled, even wider, with his freshly flossed teeth, in his mind, gleaming in the sunlight dribbling through the window, and said, "Oh yes, I found quite a good bathroom."

"Allow me to introduce the other members of the Council," the woman said, turning her eyes back down to that parchment before her, picking up her quill again and scribbling something else there.

Bert wondered if him having bathed was an important thing to note for the Council.

The woman continued, "Councilman Jebby, Marth, and Coonsoil."

Bert looked them over. All slightly wrinkled-looking old gnomes with their beards trimmed back almost to invisibility.

They all wore smart-fitting suits, and ties, and they raised their hands in a regal wave as each of them acknowledged him.

Their suits were clearly new enough that they still fit.

"Then," the woman continued, "Councilwoman Gunea, Kiis-law, and Herendashaw."

Bert now turned his attention to the female members of the Council, all of them dressed, much like the woman who spoke, in trouser suits, all of similar fit and of the same dim shades of colours.

On instinct, he looked back to the woman at the head of the

table, and the only gnome in the room who was yet to be introduced.

The smile seemed to sliver off her lips as she said, "And allow me to introduce myself, Chairwoman Maxine."

Bert felt his throat close up. He tried to swallow but couldn't.

Though he'd heard what she'd said, he was having a little difficulty in believing it.

This woman, the one who'd shepherded him off to go see Master Yorn the day before, *she* was the Chairwoman of the Council?

His mind filled with questions.

Just what had she been doing there?

Surely that was a secretary's job, an *assistant's* job?

. . . But no, he'd heard her just fine.

The woman, Chairwoman Maxine, apparently, turned the page of her parchment, cleared her throat and then glanced up to him briefly. "Right then, Mr Mhyresgnome, shall we cut to the quick?"

GETTING IT TOGETHER

AS ALWAYS, Bert had a wad of fudge tucked into the inside pocket of his jacket, but he couldn't allow himself to reach for it, however much he'd have liked to get a bit of a sugar rush going, just to take his mind off the tension that seemed to be pressing down on him.

He could still just about taste the trace of its sugar on his tongue if he thought about it a little harder.

The room seemed a little stuffy now, and he could smell the slight salty tang of sweat in the room, all of it mixed up with a touch of cologne: all sorts of fragrances from dewy-grass to smoky-lavender . . . what he knew about those fragrances was that they were supposed to give him the thought of *money*.

Everything seemed to be silent, almost holding court for him in the room, and he couldn't quite seem to keep himself focussed on any one thing.

His attention kept dwindling beyond him.

He'd thought of this moment for, well, a very *long* time really, and now it was finally here he couldn't get his ideas straight.

He breathed in deep, trying to sap whatever fresh air he could get his lungs on, and then he focussed on that killer stare of Chairwoman Maxine.

It was easy to get lost in those black pits she had for eyes— almost like he was staring right down into his mineshaft back home. But he kept hold of them and reminded himself of the most important thing to get straight.

The very issue which had led him out away from his day-to-day life for the first time in his life, and wandering off down here to see the Council.

His mouth tasted dry and he half thought about asking for some water, but decided that he'd wasted enough time already in sitting here and looking like a right lemon.

"Look," he said, then wondered if there was some sort of a ceremonial address he was meant to use when speaking to the Council, but since no one said anything to him, he guessed there wasn't . . . either that or they saw him as such a country bumpkin that they forgave him his unrefined manners, "I've paid my taxes all my life and, well, I love my Domain—I love the *Dwinns*."

This was greeted with a slight grumble of agreement from some of the male members of the council. For a second Bert thought that one of them might have a question, but, seeing they didn't, he just carried on.

"And, as I wrote in several of the letters that I attached to my tax returns, I've always had this very, uh, *moral* conscience, which is to say that I, uh, have always wanted to see some things change for the better—for the benefit of society."

Already, looking about the table, he could see some members of the Council's eyes glazing over.

When he looked back to Chairwoman Maxine, still scribbling away at her parchment, he caught her lips moving. And only then thought to listen to the words she was just about mumbling under her breath. "Mr Mhyresgnome, if this is about a hand-out, or whatever, or a tax refund, then I think . . ."

Bert held up his hand. Lifted a smile. "No, no," he said, "you've got it all wrong, see, what I'm looking for, what I've come here for is to see if you believe any of my ideas might have merit, if there might be something I can offer up for the good of society." He managed to widen his smile, but didn't think that it was any more convincing than before. "I've enough money, thanks, really, enough to keep me going for as long as I live . . . but my interests are purely political ones, in assuring the future lives of gnomes, for years to come, you see . . ."

"Excuse me," Chairwoman Maxine said, pressing her hands together, and pursing her lips. "If you wouldn't mind really coming down to what it is that you're proposing?"

Bert sucked in some more air, got himself together, and then said, "Defence."

"Defence?" she said.

"Yes."

She glanced about the other members of the Council, speaking to them only through her eyes in that way that only gnomes who know one another well can actually pull off.

That done, she looked back to Bert. "And what would the Dwinns need by way of defence?"

Bert looked at them all, a slight disbelief entering his mind now, thinking on just what it was that Lax had told him, and almost unable to believe that a callow blacksmith could know more than a roomful of, apparently, the most powerful gnomes in the Domain.

"Well, what if someone tries to invade?" Bert said, trying to stay calm.

Chairwoman Maxine brushed away this concern with one of those trademarked plain-faced smiles of hers. "The Dwinns hasn't seen combat, well, since *ever*," she said.

"But," Bert said, growing more exasperated by the second, "haven't you heard the news—of the evacuations, of villagers fleeing out of terror?"

This time he managed to elicit a couple of murmured comments among the gnomes of the Council, but whenever Bert tried to meet a murmurer's eye, they quickly looked away from him, getting awfully interested in either the sunlit rooftops outside, or one of those dingy oil paintings hanging off the wall.

Chairwoman Maxine kept up that infuriating smile of hers. "In any case, we have a moat, and we have a *wall*." She straightened out her expression a touch then continued, "Mr Mhyresgnome, really, I can't say that I quite grasp your statements and it holds that this Council must now ask that you consider the matter closed."

When Bert spoke again, he felt like his eyes were about to bulge clear out of their sockets. As far as he knew they did. "We're under attack!" he said, shouting now. "You must have heard something! If we don't mobilise now, if we don't put a little of that tax money to good use then we'll be thwarted, don't you see?"

No response from anyone in the room now.

All the councillors just kept plain faces.

No eye contact for him either.

Bert wondered back to what Master Yorn had said, about how he'd soon understand why the Dwinns had remained so backward, why the Domain had stayed so naïve in the face of the progress of the rest of the world . . . yes, it hit him now, these gnomes, these *councillors*, surely they'd . . . they'd been conspiring over this for years.

That *had* to be the explanation, the only one he could come up with.

But why?

That was the question.

Bert looked about the room, back to Chairwoman Maxine.

"Mr Mhyresgnome," she said, now scratching away at that parchment of hers once more, "though it might be true that the Dwinns does not possess so much as a single *bow* or an *arrow*, you should understand that the power of the state is quite mighty. Indeed, that little mining operation of yours—that craggy shack you keep on that hillside—we would be perfectly in our rights to take that all away."

Bert tried not to allow those comments to wind him up, because he saw that that was now her strategy. All at once, he saw the real enemy in all of this, and he wondered how he hadn't recognised it for so long.

Had he really spent all his time with his nose buried in the gloom of a mineshaft, never able to bring himself to look at the Dwinns, to see it for what it really was, to see that the way that things worked wasn't just a *fluke*?

No, it was clear to him now.

Things were the way they were because those in power—the

Council—had some sort of a stake in how they ran . . . what that stake was, he hadn't a clue.

Out in the corridor, off over his shoulder, Bert heard that steady and unmistakable tread of boots. And he knew that the guards were on their way.

Better to preserve his dignity.

And to keep his intentions from discovery.

So, with a mild, "Thank you," he turned on his heel, threw open the oak doors, and allowed the guards to march him off, out of the building, and down the steps.

When he turned back, tried to look the guards in the eye, they wouldn't even grant him so much as that.

So, with a heavy heart, he trudged on back to the hotel.

BEST-LAID PLANS, AND ALL THAT

TAKING EVERYTHING INTO ACCOUNT, Ardull couldn't say that he could've conspired for a better day to launch his attack on Cormersbarn. The sun made the dewy, long grasses glisten, and there was a light breeze in the air. Just breathing this place in, he could feel himself being dragged back to nature, as if he might all of a sudden sprout roots from his feet, and leaves from his fingers. Yes, it was certainly days like these that made him feel glad to be alive.

A pity, really, all things considered, that work was going to get in the way of his enjoyment of it.

Because he had things to do.

Towns to overthrow.

Arrive and Occupy.

After the morning inspection, going over his troops, checking their guns were all shiny and loaded, that sort of thing, he retired to his quarters and, with a slight heaviness in his heart, found Jeorge waiting for him outside the flap of his tent.

Jeorge, just like the rest of his soldiers, was lugging a rifle down at his side, and had clearly given his boots a good polish the night before. He'd trimmed his beard, too, though Ardull had a gentle feeling that that might've just been an effort to placate him further . . . before delivering yet more of that Bad News Jeorge spent so much of his life attracting.

"Sir," Jeorge said, giving a curt salute with a couple of his fingers at his temple.

Ardull gave him an equally curt nod, without meeting his eye and wandered in through the flap of his tent. "At ease."

Jeorge followed him inside. "Sir?"

Ardull couldn't help letting loose a sigh as he pawed about over his maps, and other bits and bobs, looking for another bag of yaltas leaves. "Yes?" he said, failing *not* to sound like a thoroughly bothered parent.

"Today's advance," Jeorge said.

"What about it?"

"Uh, uh, I was just thinking, sir."

"Thinking?"

"Yes, well, actually, I spent a good amount of the night thinking about it, sir."

Ardull uncovered an empty bag, bereft of any yaltas, not even those crumbly remains of leaves, nothing so much as to suck from the bottom of it.

He gave another sigh and then pawed through his trunk.

Nothing there either.

Becoming increasingly desperate, the dryness in his mouth

now becoming unbearable, he turned on Jeorge. "You, uh, don't happen to have any more of those leaves on you, do you, boy?"

Jeorge blinked a couple of times, apparently thrown off whatever it was that he had to say. "No, sir, I . . . I can't say I do."

Ardull balled his fingers into fists, slammed them against his thighs, and let loose a "Damn!" before he could think to contain himself.

"Sir?" Jeorge said.

"What?!"

"I didn't want to say anything, sir, before I mean, but I have noticed, over the past few weeks, you know, ever since we found those leaves, that you've formed, well, a . . ."

"An *addiction*!" Ardull said. "Yes, yes, I *know* that, don't you think that I can *see* that?"

"Sir, that's just . . ."

"Look, if you haven't got any more of the bloody leaves then you might as well clear out right now! Don't you think you've embarrassed your superior enough for one day, for goodness' sake?!"

Jeorge started doing that rapid-blinking thing that showed he was somewhat affronted and, undoubtedly, that his mind was racked with some sort of problem that he just couldn't see his way to keeping to himself.

Ardull breathed a couple of times. Took in the stale air of the tent, that slightly dusty, musky scent of the place, just about covered up by the lashings of cologne he'd splashed all over the fabric of the tent at various times and places.

"Go on," Ardull said, "what's the matter?"

"Well, sir," Jeorge said, the words tumbling out of his mouth the way that made Ardull think that whoever had invented the phrase 'verbal diarrhoea' had really been onto something, "it's really quite similar to your *own* predicament, sir."

Ardull felt his chest tighten and his blood slop slower through his veins, as if his heart was tired of doing its job, as if it felt like the rest of his body had clear given up on it. Feeling insanely *heavy* all of a sudden, Ardull slumped down onto his bunk, listening to the slight *creak* of the springs as he did so.

Instinctively, he brought his fingertips up to his temples and began to massage.

Oh what he wouldn't give to have his wife with him now, she always gave him the best massages, could find ways to calm him down no matter how fraught the day was or how grotty he happened to be feeling.

"What?" Ardull said, his voice croaky and distant now, and thoroughly fed up. "What's the matter *now?*"

Jeorge stood there, in the entrance to his tent and looked shy all of a sudden, as if he realised just how drawn-out Ardull was now, and was conscious of laying just another annoying thing on top of him.

"Go *on!*" Ardull said, hinting to Jeorge that he could still lose his temper despite his fatigue, despite all the drug-addled stuff going on inside his poor gnomish body.

"The men," Jeorge said, "they've . . . they've, well, you should really come and see, sir."

Ardull couldn't quite get his head around it.

If there was one thing that he just couldn't stand, it was enigmas. He liked things laid out plainly for him. Like the prose he set down on the page: for everything to be crisp and free from *enigma*.

Anyway, what could possibly have happened? He'd only just

got back from inspecting his soldiers, and they'd all been in tip-top shape, all of them ready to go and carry out the orders that they'd come all this way to put into action.

"Sir?"

Ardull propped himself up with his elbow, and then, taking it slow, helped himself up to his feet, telling himself that if this turned out to be one of those normal problems of Jeorge's, which was to say a *stupid* problem, then he would personally decapitate him.

That would show any of those smirking gnomes who might doubt his poetical, *passionate* soul.

He would set them all right.

And so, at a loping trudge, he followed on out on Jeorge's too-spritely boot heels, and out of his tent to see the soldiers all before him.

All dressed up in their uniforms, their brass buttons gleaming in the morning sunlight, and the creases in their trousers casting sharp shadows, the soldiers were all in various poses of melee.

Fighting one another.

Wrestling on the ground.

Holding punch-ups in ragged circles.

It was a mess.

A total mess.

Ardull looked back at Jeorge. "And this is all because of those *bloody* leaves?"

Jeorge nodded, a touch glumly, but also, Ardull was *sure*, with just a little smugness.

Because Ardull knew well that Jeorge hadn't so much as *touched* the yaltas leaves.

And the whole irony of it was, now with his soldiers driven

half crazy, fighting *one another*, Jeorge was the only one that he could truly trust.

Ardull wondered how long it would be before he'd descend into that same sort of maddening rage . . . because he had lost any of the leaves he'd had . . . how long might he have: a day, two days?

Was he beginning to crack now?

With a harsh sigh, Ardull turned on his heel and returned to his tent, giving Jeorge orders to let him know when his gnomes had managed to shake off their withdrawal symptoms.

It looked like the plan of attack for today was truly scuppered.

Bugger.

YOU TRY TO DO A GOOD THING AND LOOK WHAT HAPPENS

BERT DIDN'T CARE that he woke Lax from his sleep by slamming the bedroom door on his way back from the visit to the Council. He could feel the blood frothing through his veins, and his heart trying its hardest to bounce up into his throat. As soon as he'd got the building of the Seat out of sight, he'd shoved in a great big mess of fudge past his lips, and he chewed it up now, feeling the sugar already seep into his bloodstream.

The room smelled a little of sweat, and that same fermentation from the night before, and also of other gnomic gasses that he didn't care to think about right now.

It was also staggeringly warm—*baking* almost.

As he whipped about the room, gathering his things, shoving his clothing back into his knapsack, he threw a glance over his shoulder, to Lax, who was either coming around from sleeping or was having some awfully vivid, and *talkative*, dream.

Lax *was* awake, as it turned out, though his eyes looked extremely bleary and it seemed like the back of his hand had become surgically attached to his forehead during the night. "Wha . . . wha . . ."

"Don't worry," Bert said, cutting him off. "You didn't miss anything. I just went to go and see a roomful of numbskulls— didn't learn anything new except this whole business of coming here was a gigantic waste of time."

Lax flapped his lips, and it wasn't quite clear if it was out of confusion or out of a genuine attempt to say something.

In any case, Bert pushed him aside once more. "Look, I'm sorry about your village, about you not being able to find anyone, but this is the end of it for me. I'm just going to head on back, crawl back into my mansion and see out my days very happy with my accumulated wealth, thank you very much. It was a mistake me coming here. Just a *big* mistake."

This time Lax did manage to get some words out. "We . . . we *going* then?"

Bert nodded his head, and might well have frothed at the mouth if he hadn't had company. "Yes we *are* bloody well going!"

Lax mumbled something and Bert guessed that it was something along the lines of him agreeing to come with him, at least Lax started shifting about on the bed, scrunching up the bed sheets, yawning and stretching.

Blinking the sleep from his eyes.

Bert did up the wooden toggles on his knapsack and then hurled the damn thing over his shoulder. He stood and looked over to Lax, seeing that, still rubbing the sleep from his eyes, he was prodding his feet into his rugged boots having apparently slept in his overalls.

Lax cast a glance over at Bert. "Where . . . where're we going now?"

Bert let loose a sigh. He thought about what he'd already said, about how he was going to return to his mansion, just forget he'd ever come here in the first place. And if those stories about there being some sorts of invaders in the Dwinns came to pass then he'd quite happily turn himself over to them.

Now he saw exactly what Master Yorn had hinted at the day before . . . and he wished that he'd taken his laughter in a better way, realised that, in its own way, it had been a warning of just what he intended to do . . . about just how numbskulled all the members of the Council were, how unlikely they were to listen to reason.

Knapsack hanging from his shoulder, Bert sucked up all the musty, sweaty—not to mention *fermented*—air of the room, and then met Lax's child-gnome eyes. "You tell me," he said. "What the hell are we supposed to do now?"

Lax managed to stumble his way upwards, into a standing position. His red beard had gone all curly, and had various pieces of things that Bert really had no intention of investigating any further . . . but he was pretty certain one of said pieces pertained to a gherkin, or what had *once been* a gherkin.

Lax blinked another few times, apparently getting all the sharp edges of the world about him to soften just a little bit. He looked to Bert with a slight frown. "Why don't we try to find someone else in town, someone who'll listen to us?"

Bert shook his head, couldn't help a wry smile. "Oh no," he said, "not likely to happen, no thank you."

Lax frowned a little deeper. "Why's that? You've come all this way, I didn't think you'd be thrown off the scent so easily."

Bert gave him a half shrug, thought for a microsecond about telling a lie, but decided that his, apparently trusty, travelling companion deserved better. "Look," he began, "these gnomes, the *Council*"—he couldn't help *not* inflecting *that* word with a great deal of bile—"they threatened me, threatened everything that I've achieved. They don't want me to go about asking any more questions."

Lax clamped his eyes shut for several seconds, long enough for Bert to convince himself that the next thing to pass his lips would be vomit . . . but, against all odds, Lax opened his eyes again, apparently a mite steadier, and continued.

"So we're off, then?"

"Looks like it," Bert said, and then, thinking things over a little better, said, "How about we go off and look for your villagers, work out where they've got to, eh?"

At this, Lax seemed to brighten, despite his swivel-eyed hangover. "Yeah?" he said.

Bert nodded in reply. "Come on, let's get some breakfast down us first, if you think you can manage it."

As Bert made for the door, he passed by Lax and, on instinct, gave him a hearty slap between the shoulder blades.

In retrospect it was probably a bad move . . . but Lax seemed to hold himself together well enough, so to speak, and followed Bert out of the room and down to the breakfast room.

SCREW THEM ALL

W ITH A TRULY STOMACH-BUSTING breakfast of well-buttered scrambled eggs, crunchy wholemeal toast, with extra butter, and whole bucket loads of coffee . . . there was no butter in that which Bert could discern . . . they made their way out through the urban sprawl that had turned out to be Cormersbarn and headed on out to the bridges, all nice and *not* flooded now thanks to a whole day's sunshine.

Bert shifted the weight of his knapsack over to his left shoulder, and, to be honest, he couldn't have felt better. He tried out a couple of tunes, whistling them, but he soon gave up when he could almost hear the internal groans coming from behind him.

Why, Bert could remember back when he'd been a spritely forty-, or fifty-, year-old gnome, and when he'd taken in a whole stomach-load of fermented liquids, got himself thoroughly sozzled.

Though those days were behind him now, he remembered

well how his elders would somehow divine all the best ways to keep his migraine going along at full whack.

He could almost still feel those throbbing pangs of pain.

And that was just how Lax must've felt now.

So he stopped the whistling.

It was a beautiful, fresh day, and he was pleased to leave behind the smoky chimneys of Cormersbarn and to step out onto the lightly creaking planks of the bridge leading him on out over the moat and onto the swishing glade stretching out before them.

Everything out ahead seemed to be totally green. It reminded him of his hillside, back home, and when he would look out of his mansion, the other side of the valley to the village, and pretend that he was the only gnome in whole of the world.

And sometimes he could stay like that for hours.

Some days he *really* believed that he was the only gnome in the world.

They made good time, with Bert this time taking up the lead, his compass laid flat in his palm before him but hardly needed considering the well-beaten track that he soon came across, the track that they'd taken when they'd come here, to Cormersbarn, from Phardoe.

He felt the cool winds against his cheek, blowing away the sweat which oozed on out from his skin, and seeming to chill his blood.

He felt that final flex of his calf muscles, that last strain, as he stepped on over the brink of the hill which overlooked the town.

And it was then that he couldn't resist the urge to look back.

To glance over his shoulder.

For one final look at Cormersbarn.

He had no intention of ever returning.

Why would he when he had everything he needed for *his* life up in his mansion?

It just befuddled him that he'd ever thought he could make a concrete difference to the Dwinns, that he would be seen as anything other than a 'crackpot,' as Master Yorn had put it, for suggesting some sort of a change to the status quo.

He held his hand up to his brow, keeping the gleam of the sun from his eyes as he looked off over the sprawling town, and waited for Lax to catch up with him.

A blue haze rose up over the city, all those fires combined and blowing together. And he could still catch a whiff of that horse muck carrying on the breeze. Could just about make out the *clickety-clack* of the carts too. And he wondered why it was such a wild idea for them to expand the infrastructure, for them to create coach stations, rest points, so that they might unite the whole of the Dwinns with *horse*power.

But he was just a damp-eyed dreamer, he saw as much now.

And so he'd just go on back to his dreaming, back to his independent mining operation, and to his marble mansion, where he wouldn't bother anybody any longer.

Just pay his taxes and stay quiet.

As Lax cringed his way up onto the summit of the hill, Bert looked over his pallid complexion, that distinct greenness in his gills. That way his freckled cheeks and red hair seemed to accentuate those sickly features of his.

Bert wished that he might come up with something to aid

the boy's hangover but, in the end, he knew that this would just be a lesson learned.

One that Lax, most likely, wouldn't forget for some time.

When Lax got up onto the top of the hill, he doubled over, apparently not all that bothered with taking a glimpse of Cormersbarn before it slipped out of view, and *was* promptly sick.

Bert just smiled a little and tried to stand upwind of Lax, making offhand comments along the lines of, "Better out than in," and "Good lad, get it all out," before he realised, when Lax slipped him a testy sidelong glance, that he might be doing about as much good here as he'd been doing with the whistling before.

So, with a fairly contented sigh, Bert cast his final look over Cormersbarn: its acutely angled roofs, its multi-coloured tarps, and, of course, the terrific brickwork of the wall which surrounded the whole of the town.

Perhaps the Council *did* have a point after all about them not needing to fear attack. And while it was true that the Council had a duty to protect the *whole* of the Dwinns he realised now that they really had no pressing need to see through that duty.

After all, hardly anyone in the Domain paid taxes and those that did, suckers like Bert, just got themselves laughed at.

. . . Maybe it *was* time that Bert found that proverbial lady gnome and went about making gnomlings . . . perhaps the only real answer to the problem was to soak the lands with his genetic makeup, with *good, honest* genetic makeup so that future generations would be entrepreneurial and respectable.

Yes, perhaps that was the answer after—

"HANDS UP!"

A JOLT ran up Bert's spine. The voice was accented, apparently someone unused to speaking Dwindish, or someone who was good at *affecting* that they were foreign . . . though why someone would want to do such a thing escaped him.

Bert spun around, of course, as any self-respecting gnome would do at such a command. And he faced up to his apparent adversary.

The gnome was dressed in camos and carried what looked like a stick. It took him another moment to recall, from photographs he'd seen of wider Gnomelandia, that this was a gun . . . a *rifle* if he wasn't mistaken.

And this, well, from what he had seen and heard, was supposed to be something called a *soldier* . . . yes, thinking about it now that was just what he was dealing with here.

As if by a miracle, it only took another couple of seconds for the final pieces of the puzzle to slip home. All that stuff about invaders. Well, here he was. He was *looking* at one.

This gnome, though, Bert had to admit, didn't quite fit the gnomic soldiers he'd seen in photographs, which was to say that he looked a little, well, *overweight*.

Not that he was going to say anything at all about that right now.

Not with that *rifle* pointed at him.

The gnome had brown eyebrows, that looked about as out of control as those hedges at the bottom of his garden that he'd often thought about taking care of 'one of these days.'

And he had shaved the rest of his beard, just leaving a kind of moustache there.

It made him look very odd.

The soldier's rosy cheeks seemed almost in total opposition to the rest of this scene . . . but, again, Bert wasn't necessarily in a strong position to comment on this.

"Uh," Bert said, slipping a glance in Lax's direction, seeing that he was striking just about the same pose as he was . . . arms in the air, etcetera.

"Don't speak!" the gnomic soldier said, again in that clanky, foreign-sounding way.

Bert couldn't quite decide whether it was the soldier's accent or the particular tone he struck that made him sound so menacing.

The idea he took home from it all, though, was that this was a gnome on the edge, and if this gnome hadn't before had personal experience of drawing blood, he had almost certainly read an awful lot about it in books.

At the very least.

"Move!" the gnomic soldier said, jerking his rifle in the direction that he, apparently, wanted them to move in.

Bert slipped another glance to Lax, as if he was looking for some sort of cue.

All that Lax seemed to be saying to him, albeit very clearly and succinctly, was 'I'm going to be sick again.'

And—wouldn't you just know it?—he was.

The gnomic soldier struck an expression of total disgust, his lips all writhing about in a way that made the fuzz on his upper lip do a little dance, almost like a caterpillar hanging down from the strand of a spider web, flirting with freedom.

The moustache didn't break free, however.

"Are yoo quite *finish*!" the gnomic soldier said, making it sound far more like a manic command than a polite inquiry.

Though Bert was starting to get the gist that nothing about this little exchange here was going to be all that polite.

Lax straightened up and gave the gnomic soldier a doleful nod.

This seemed to satisfy the gnomic soldier.

"Now!" the gnomic soldier said. "Over *here*!"

Bert saw no reason not to do what he said, so, trudging along, hearing Lax coming along with him, he went off in the direction that the gnomic soldier indicated.

Since there were no more cries of outrage from the soldier, he supposed that he and Lax were doing just fine. And he hoped that, if they kept on doing everything the soldier said, they'd get out of this thing alive.

Or was that just wishful thinking?

PRISONERS!

ARDULL'S TEETH chattered uncontrollably. It didn't matter how tightly he clenched his jaws, the chattering wouldn't stop. It was like a bunch of worms had entered his bloodstream and were all jiggling about within him. He knew it was the fault of the yaltas leaves, of course, but what good could that knowledge do him now? There were none left.

He gripped the sides of his bunk, clinging to the wooden frame of it, and feeling his fingers draw tight about it.

His heart sounded in his throat, seemed to be making inroads on his tonsils, and he wished that he could just get himself shot of this fever that racked him.

But he knew the only way he'd do that was with a good, hearty mouthful of yaltas leaves, and there were none left, and they were now too tricky to get his hands on.

He glanced to his side, to his notebook which lay open, the

last few lines of verse he'd scrawled out there, broken off halfway into a line when the shuddering had got the better of him. Now he knew the pains of addiction. Understood the full effect it could have on his body. He knew the pain that his gnomes had felt when they'd broken out into fight among one another. Goodness, he would snap his firstborn's neck to get his hands on some yaltas.

. . . Sweat leaked out of him. When the draught billowing in through the fabric of the tent met with his skin he shuddered all the more.

Delirious. He was *really* getting delirious.

Had he really just said to himself that he would snap his first-born's neck to get some yaltas? . . . Or had he said it aloud?

Outside, he could hear boots crunching their way towards his tent.

He clasped his eyes shut and brought his fingertips up to massage his temples.

Couldn't they just leave him alone?

Wasn't it enough that the attack had been abandoned for the day?

His gnomes deemed unfit to Arrive and Occupy Corm-ersbarn.

Apparently not, because again came that approximation of a knock at the fabric of his tent. Feeling a lot like a lion with a toothache, he barked for them to come inside.

It wasn't as he expected, which was to say that Jeorge wasn't the first one to step through the doorway. The first to step through was a gnome dressed in civilian clothing. Wearing a thick jumper and with a knapsack on his back.

Another, a red-haired gnome, soon followed him.

Ardull's chattering teeth subsided for a moment, apparently just as keen to find out what this was about.

The chattering only started up again when he caught sight of Jeorge stepping on in after them. It was surely a bad sign that the mere presence of his personal assistant now had an adverse physical effect on him.

But he concentrated on the two gnomes dressed in civvies. "What've we got here?" Ardull said, vaguely in the direction of the gnomes.

Jeorge replied. "Found these two skulking about on the hill, overlooking Cormersbarn, thought I'd bring them in right away. Have a suspicious look about them, don't they?"

Ardull's eyes drifted over Jeorge, saw that he was holding his rifle, and pointing it right at his chest. He looked at him with alarm, and that seemed just enough to get Jeorge to realise just what it was he was doing.

Jeorge lifted his rifle, pointed it to the ceiling of the tent.

A much *safer* position.

Ardull helped himself up off his bunk and onto his feet which, not more than half an hour ago, hadn't allowed him to walk so much as a step straight.

Now, though, he felt more assured, and maybe it was just through pure force of will that he managed to keep himself upright. That he managed to strut on up to the two gnomes.

"Dwindians," Ardull said, almost to himself.

The two gnomes.

The *prisoners* nodded to him.

Ardull brought his hand up, miraculously not shaking, and he rested it in the pit of his chin. He didn't speak any Dwindish and, to his knowledge, neither did Jeorge.

Nothing beyond the basics, anyway.

As if Jeorge was thinking just the same thing, he nodded to Ardull and then slipped on out of the tent, the sounds of his boots drifting away.

Ardull narrowed his eyes and looked the gnomes over, scoping them out.

The one that stood a little further forwards, the one with the blond hair, he looked a little older. Had that leathered skin that only came with age, and experience.

Though what possible experience a Dwindian could cook up escaped him.

He guessed the blond gnome to be well into his mid-hundreds.

Now, the other one, the one with the red hair, the one who looked like he was on the brink of being very ill indeed, he was much younger.

Maybe in his mid-forties, perhaps fifties.

He'd always been good at telling ages.

Something that had served him very well in his poetry.

Or at least that was how he liked to look at it.

It was only as Ardull heard the returning boot steps that he thought to speak, thought to sort of hint at relieving the tension that lurked over the inside of his tent.

"Now," Ardull said, "your Domain shall fall."

HUH?

BERT REALLY COULDN'T make head or tail of just what this uniformed gnome was saying to him. He was still taken a little off guard by all the shining medals he had sticking out from the lapel of his dark green jacket, and the way that he seemed to constantly wear a smirk.

He'd also caught sight of that notebook over at the side of his bunk, and though he didn't read so much as a word of Juttilian, he could tell it when he heard it, and he knew just by the form of the writing on the notebook pages that it was poetry.

A warrior poet.

How quaint.

As Bert breathed in the musky air—air that truly put the air in the room they'd stayed in last night to shame with its sweatiness and the faintly noble attempts to cover it up with cologne—he heard the footsteps outside.

The returning gnomic soldier, along with another set of footsteps.

What did they have planned here?

What did they want from them?

Bert could feel a block of fudge in the breast pocket of his tunic, and he had to resist all those jangling urges to reach for it —to stuff it between his lips.

He could only imagine the slick sugary taste.

Could only imagine the comforting warmth that would glow through his blood.

All things considered, Lax looked like he might be more in need of a decent square of fudge than him. If Bert knew one thing about pale complexions it was that it often meant low blood sugar.

And fudge would take just great care of that.

No time now, though, because the gnomic soldier stepped on in through the flap of the tent, along with another gnome, one who wore a blue-and-black striped jumper that looked like it hadn't been washed for a good week, the way that it seemed pretty much held together with stains of various colours and consistencies.

And that was a little bizarre what with the lint all springing up off the jumper too, making it look, conversely, that it had been washed perhaps once too often.

The jumpered gnome wore a silver stud earring.

Bert couldn't help noticing the grimace that the uniformed gnome put on when he cast his glance over the jumpered gnome, and they babbled on in Juttilian, apparently some sort of a discussion taking place.

Bert didn't see that there was a problem here, but, then

again, he really had no idea what was going on at all.

Finally, the babbling stopped and the jumpered gnome turned to Bert first. He licked his full, purple lips and gave him a wry smile. "What is your name?" he said, his accent near perfect, just with a slight chop to its tone.

Bert guessed that this gnome's first language was Juttilian but he'd surely spent no small amount of blood and sweat trying to get his Dwindish sounding decent enough.

Bert told him his name.

The jumpered gnome had a little trouble pronouncing his surname.

It seemed that, for Juttilians, Mhyresgnome just wasn't one of those names that tripped off the tongue.

The jumpered gnome gave up after a couple of valiant efforts, not bothering to ask Lax for his name, only giving him a somewhat afterthought of a glance before turning his attention back to Bert. "You have come from Cormersbarn, yes?"

Bert shook his head. "No, we were just visiting."

As he replied, he noticed the uniformed gnome and the gnomic soldier both leaning into them as if they might be able to understand better if they were a little closer.

The jumpered gnome translated for them.

Until that moment, Bert hadn't truly appreciated just how ugly a language Juttilian was.

Really, it was like listening to someone sucking on a drainpipe full of mulch.

The jumpered gnome licked his lips again, smiled a little more wryly, as if he was on the cusp of some brilliant breakthrough. "Then," the jumpered gnome said, meeting Bert's eyes, "what were you doing in Cormersbarn?"

Bert wondered whether he should tell the whole truth or just prod at it.

Maybe it was that he was just so thoroughly fed up with everything that had happened, or maybe he was tired from the trek down here, along the hills, to this Juttilian encampment.

Or perhaps he just wasn't thinking all that straight.

But the first was the most likely.

Revenge, he'd always found, was only ever second to being able to tell someone 'I told you so.'

"I went to go see the Gnomish Council of the Dwinns," he said, as if he was tossing a . . . now what had that thing been called? . . . a *hand* grenade, that was it!

Sometimes he wondered if he'd been born into the wrong Domain.

When the jumpered gnome translated, it had just the reaction that he'd hoped for, which was to say that there were an awful lot of exchanged glances and gawping expressions and widening eyes.

This time the uniformed officer swept the jumpered gnome aside, met Bert's eyes with his own and then said, in slow, almost *painfully* slow, Dwindish. "You. Must. Tell. All."

Bert glanced to Lax, saw that he was looking more frail by the second.

Which was to say that the way things were going this tent floor might not be vomit-free for much longer.

Bert sucked in as much air as he could through his mouth, so that he wouldn't have to breathe the clamouring and overwhelmingly *stinky* odour of the tent.

Then he told them everything he knew.

AND RELAX

I T FELT GOOD to get it all out of him. It was like when he found a blister between his toes, found that throbbing, bulged-up bit of nastiness sticking to him. Could feel it welling up and almost taking on a life of its own, like it might, in the middle of the night, break free completely of his skin and simply bounce on out the window and to a new life.

Spilling everything he knew, every single lingering doubt, every pent-up sense of injustice about the way that the Dwinns functioned . . . why, it felt just as good as taking a searing hot needle to said blister.

Though he wasn't sure how, he found himself, as the discussion was winding itself up, sitting down on the edge of the bunk in the tent, with the jumpered gnome, the uniformed gnome, and the gnomic soldier all looking at him with great, big eyes.

It was like something traumatic had happened to him and they were doing their best to console him.

Then again, he did supposed that, all things considered, it really *had* been a bit of a traumatic lifetime . . . not to be *overly* dramatic about the whole thing.

Gnomelandia was supposed to be second only to paradise, after all.

It was only when Bert opened his mouth, when he met the jumpered gnome's eyes and prepared his next line of bile that he realised that he had nothing else to say.

He had told them everything.

He wondered how long they'd been there.

How long they'd stood around listening to him gush forth.

When he looked beyond them, to the side of the tent, he saw Lax all slumped up there, fast asleep, a little bubble of drool perpetually growing and then shrinking as he breathed his deep breaths.

Granted, it couldn't have taken all that much of an opportunity for Lax to get a decent kip in, but it looked like he'd been there for a good old time.

The jumpered gnome had his mouth slightly latched open still, as if he was expecting more from Bert, or maybe he was just reeling from the sheer quantity of information that Bert had spilled so willingly.

Bert had never imagined that he'd be a traitor to his Domain, but, then again, he'd never really thought that he'd ever be in the position to be one.

And now that he'd found himself in that position it had just seemed the logical step.

Anyway, these guys didn't seem all that bad. He had always thought that he was good at judging gnomes, and these ones—aside from being foreign—seemed to be in-and-out okay to him.

When the jumpered gnome gathered that Bert had nothing more to say, he smiled that wry *wry* smile yet again, his silver earring glinting a little in the dim light of the tent, and then he turned and conferred with the uniformed gnome and the gnomic soldier.

They turned their backs to Bert, rather rudely he thought, and spoke in hushed tones though Bert really hadn't a hope in hell of understanding so much as a snatched word of Juttilian. It was one thing to look at it all written out on a page and another to attempt to get even the most basic grasp of its sweeps and turns off the tongue.

Let alone the gnashings of the teeth.

Bert could tell that the uniformed gnome, the older gnome with all the medals pinned to his chest, was the one in charge, just from the way that he thrust his finger in just about everyone's noses. If he wasn't careful he was going to put out an eye with that thing.

Whatever it was that the uniformed gnome was saying it was passionate and he definitely believed himself right.

It was strange to see him almost arguing with himself, because surely he wasn't going to have any resistance from either of the other two gnomes—they were clearly inferiors to him.

But Bert guessed that, more than anything else, the uniformed gnome was just trying to convince himself of something . . . thinking about that notebook full of poetry he'd spied off lying beside the uniformed officer's bunk, he guessed that there was a bit of a sensitive soul lurking away in the otherwise stainless-steel exterior.

A 'heart of gold' was what they called it.

. . . Yeah, Bert guessed that he probably had one of those too.

Why else would he have come down here, come to Cormers-barn, to make a fool of himself?

The uniformed gnome broke off the deliberations fairly soon after Lax released just about the mightiest, rib-ticklingliest snore Bert had ever had the misfortune to experience.

It actually sent a shudder up Bert's spine, and the three Juttilian gnomes spinning around as if they thought it might be some sort of a . . . what was its name? . . . artillery shell?

Bert couldn't help but allow himself a smile. Though he hadn't had all that much experience with war, or fighting of any kind. In fact, come to think of it, he'd had *no* experience whatsoever of it. He could quite clearly see that these three gnomes were quite tightly wired, as if they were all ready to explode at the brush of a fingernail.

And he found himself wondering just how much action they'd seen between them.

Maybe not as much as their confidence suggested.

The three gnomes, with the uniformed gnome at the front, peered down at Bert.

For some reason, Bert got the feeling that this might well be the moment of truth here, staring him in the face.

The uniformed gnome spoke rapid-fire Juttilian to the jumpered / translator gnome, who passed on the message to Bert. "We want to know if you will fight on beside us, if you shall join us in the operation to seize control of Cormersbarn."

ULTIMATUM

BERT THOUGHT THIS OVER. It wasn't quite a question, or a request even, it was just a kind of plea for knowledge, for him to let them know just where he stood. Something about this sounded very much 'take it or leave it.'

Better to get that cleared up first.

And so, without batting an eyelid he said, "What if I don't fight with you?"

The jumpered gnome had no need to translate the reply or to ask advice from his superior officer. Not so much as a nod passed between the two of them. The jumpered gnome simply said, "You shall be shot."

Bert glanced off behind them to where Lax slept on, unperturbed by these events. Bert thought he saw a decent strategy to buy just a little time. "Uh, what about my friend, does he have to fight too?"

The jumpered gnome nodded vigorously, again without

needing to discuss the matter with his superior. Come to think of it, that was probably what they'd been thrashing out when they'd been discussing things just a little while ago.

Bert weighed up the matter.

It wasn't like he had *all* that much to live for, taking *everything* into account. Sure, he had his material wealth, his mansion, his *ideals* . . . though they'd now been thoroughly trampled on . . .

But that was it, wasn't it?

Wasn't the whole thing here an opportunity?

Only one way to find out.

"Erm," Bert said, three sets of eyes glaring at him, waiting for his response, "Just what sort of a society are you thinking of putting into place in Cormersbarn—I mean, when you go through with this 'Arrive-and-Occupy' plan?"

This time the jumpered gnome did have to consult with his superior, though it was a fairly succinct dialogue that terminated in a curt nod from the uniformed gnome.

"Uh," the jumpered gnome said, "we'd work at creating . . . how should I say? . . . a more *modern* society."

Bert thought about this for a moment then said, "I've noticed that you don't have any horses."

"No," the jumpered gnome said, then consulted quickly with the uniformed officer before adding, "we lost them all in bogs, and deserts, you see, on our way here."

That *did* change matters just a little.

In fact, the way that this exchange of ideas had gone, Bert could quite clearly see an agreement on the choppy horizon . . . closer, actually, perhaps lapping in with the tide. "Would you, uh, care to listen to some of my proposals if the operation is a success and if I, uh, fight quite *bravely*?"

"Yes," the jumpered gnome said, "we would listen."

Now this really was sounding promising, indeed.

Modern infrastructure . . . well, horse-drawn carts threaded about the Domain would be a start, and he guessed that the Juttilians would have all sorts of other ideas that they'd quite willingly bring with them, why he wondered if he should ask them about tax—

"Answer!" the uniformed gnome said, nostrils flared, and voice booming.

The briskness of the command startled Bert quite a bit. But he didn't let it get to him completely. He knew that he was still very much the one in charge of his, and Lax's, fate here . . . come to think of it perhaps he should go and wake him up, it was probably quite bad form for him to be making such life-altering decisions without his say-so.

Then again, the uniformed gnome did look mighty intimidating and Bert wasn't quite sure how he'd handle a polite request to squeeze past and go to consult his sleeping partner.

Actually, he did have some idea.

From the looks of those dark circles beneath the uniformed officer's eyes, and the way that every vein in his neck seemed to be throbbing with thick, muscular blood, he would probably take Bert's head off right here and now, and damn the mess.

"Well?" the jumpered gnome said, sounding just a touch anxious, worried about what his own superior might do to Bert if he didn't give an answer in a timely fashion.

There really wasn't anything more to think about, and that—

"ANSWER!" the uniformed gnome said again.

Bert glanced over to Lax, gave the faintest of polite smiles and then looked the uniformed gnome back in the eye. "Fine," he said. "Yes, we'll fight with you."

The effect of Bert's words was like turning the release valve on a pipe of gushing hot water . . . which is to say that there was quite a bit of steam floating about the place.

Bert was surprised that the tent didn't lift off the ground like a hot air balloon.

Then again, he guessed that they used some very sturdy and, no doubt, very *modern* tent pegs to keep it fastened to the ground.

A BIT OF A CONFIDENCE BOOSTER

T HOUGH ARDULL'S THROAT was a touch sore from all the shouting, he could hardly believe his luck, could hardly believe that Jeorge had finally come good, that he had actually brought him something of use instead of constantly babbling on about problems that didn't need his micromanaging.

The two Dwindians that Jeorge had brought it had given him absolutely *priceless* information.

Well, *one* of them had.

And, to be fair, he had already known just how useless the defences at Cormersbarn were, but now he had absolute proof that they were incompetent too, that the gnomes running the Dwinns hadn't the first clue about what they were doing.

Even their own gnomes were frustrated with them.

What puzzled him, though, was that no one seemed to be doing anything about it.

In fact, once he'd finally cracked through the one called

Flaughterbert's outer shell he'd got the distinct impression that the gnome clearly wanted to actively help them with their operation, and then it had been down to Ardull to spell out the deal, down to him to let the gnome know just what he was getting himself in for.

Treason . . . what did it really mean?

Ardull ceased his constant marching back and forth through his tent, and—*damn it!*—he had his hands clutched at his lower back yet again. Anyone who might've been watching so much as his silhouette on the outside of the tent would've had no doubts in their minds that he was a real villain.

But he wasn't.

He was only an artist earning a living.

Doing whatever his bosses told him to do.

He turned around, his mouth now impossibly dry from all the shouting, but at least the excitement and anticipation of the coming operation lifted his spirits just a little, and took his mind off those yaltas leaves.

His notebook sat opened beside his bunk on the groundsheet of the tent. He wondered if the Dwindian gnomes had seen it, and he felt his throat squeeze tight, his blood pound to his temples at the horror of it.

But, once that initial reaction had passed, he got to wondering, if the Dwindian gnomes *had* in fact seen it, and *had* in fact understood it, whether or not they'd thought it was any good. He could ask them, he supposed, but what would their opinion mean?

He'd threatened them with death if they failed to cooperate with him.

And though neither of them would be carrying a weapon

with them, they'd be extremely useful throughout the operation, and be excellent guides to help them get into the town.

And maybe useful as leverage when Ardull brought his forces to confront the Council.

That gnome, that *Flaughterbert* gnome, had claimed that he had met personally with Council, and Ardull never missed an opportunity to have just a little dialogue up his sleeve.

Because he sure as hell couldn't speak Dwindish worth a damn.

Ardull stood still for a few moments, brought his hands back from where he'd been writhing them at the base of his spine. He looked them over. Good hands. Slightly leathered. Working hands . . . a poet's hands?

He caught the notebook out of the corner of his eye once more, that half finished line. That had been bothering him for hours and hours now, he just hadn't seemed able to complete it. Maybe now, though, maybe now that his mind was a little clearer, now that the cravings for yaltas leaves were letting him rest.

He stooped down, picked up his notebook, read the lines once again:

A new dawn, a new hope,
Rivers flow refreshed,
Enemies sleep in their beds,
And a land, a land awaits, . . .

He racked his brains, trying to come up with just the right turn of phrase. Those last lines, it was *always* those last lines that did his head in, that had the beating of him till he woke in the middle of the night with the answer on his mind finally . . . and he would shuck his bed sheets, scrabble out of bed and scribble it down in a frenzy.

But now, the last line . . . he tapped his pencil against the spiral rings of the notebook, tried to get himself to think a little straighter.

He brought the pencil up to his beard, coiled a couple of strands of hair about the end of it, deep in thought.

Yes . . . yes . . . *yes!*

He had it.

Exactly.

Right there, at the front of his mind.

On the tip of his tongue.

And on the lead of his pencil.

He returned to the verse, and added:

It awaits to be conquered.

SLEEPING OUT

BERT HAD EXPECTED to be sleeping out under the stars tonight, but if someone had told him that he'd be deep within enemy territory . . . or, well, *supposed* enemy territory, then he probably would've laughed at them out of hand.

. . . And yet, here he was, lying on his bunk with the snoring Lax alongside him, and the clear night sky up above them—stars all twinkling down.

A pair of gnomic guards stood close by, chatting about twenty paces away from them, a candle glowing between them, and their cotton-wool beards catching the light like optical fibres . . . was that the stuff he'd read about . . . the stuff that could just about pump any sort of information about the place at the blink of an eye?

Or was it just a fairy tale?

Sometimes it was difficult to know the difference here, in the Dwinns.

Tomorrow they would return to Cormersbarn but this time Bert would have reinforcements, gnomes who wanted to shift the paradigm for good . . . make life all the better in the Dwinns, hoik the place, kicking and screaming, out of the Dark Ages, and into the Modern Age.

To think that when he'd heard the jumpered gnome, the one doing the translating, confirm for him that they did *indeed* have horses, that had set a warmth glowing at the pit of Bert's chest, and yet, at the same time, he knew just how silly it was.

After all, horses weren't any advanced technology.

They'd been around for ages.

And yet the Gnomish Council of the Dwinns had never thought of putting together the very basics involved in transport infrastructure.

He really had no idea why he'd gone after them about defence now, because that was what the Dwinns least needed . . . the Dwinns only needed to be taken over by gnomes who actually knew what they were doing.

It took Bert a little off guard when he glanced to his side, saw Lax with his eyes wide open, glinting in the bare moonlight that beamed down on them. He hadn't noticed that he'd stopped his snoring, but he was pretty glad about it.

"Recovered?" Bert said.

Lax managed a slight smile. "I think so."

Bert smiled back at him and then flipped over on his back, feeling the ribs of his camping bunk poking into his spine. He could lose himself so easily in the pitch-black sky which swooped out above them. It was hard to believe that out and beyond Gnomelandia there were other worlds, other planets all set for exploring.

And here he was, stuck down here in the Dwinns without so much as a horse and cart to travel between villages.

"You worried about tomorrow?" Lax said.

Bert thought about it for a moment, felt his chest tighten a little, but didn't let on anything in the tone of his reply. "Nah," Bert said, "the Dwinns is toothless now—nothing to it at all . . . we'll march on in there, the Juttilians will take it over and then, before you know it, we'll all be living in a truly modern society."

"Y'think?"

"I hope so," Bert said, with a sigh, "otherwise this whole quest will have been a massive waste of time, won't it?"

"Hmm."

When Bert slipped Lax a sidelong glance he saw that he was also lying on his back, staring up at the night sky, and no doubt considering those same deep questions that all gnomes had considered to themselves since the dawning of all creation . . . whenever that had actually been.

"It's the right thing, isn't it?" Lax said.

"I think so."

"I mean, it just seems weird what we're doing, you know, siding with the enemy, or the gnomes that we've been told are the enemy."

"That's because it *is* weird," Bert said, "but what's more weird is the way that the Dwinns are set up so that we have no choice in the matter—how else can we get what we need from our Domain if those that're in charge are complete idiots?"

Lax breathed a sigh and when he spoke again his voice was hardly above a whisper—so quiet that Bert couldn't be sure that he'd spoken at all. "Patience," he said.

Bert turned that word over in his mind.

Patience.

A good, trusty old word.

One that'd served him well in his mining business, if in no other walk of life.

Yes, *patience*.

. . . And there was a time for patience, a time to send off letter after letter, year after year, with the very best intentions at heart.

And then there was that time to get laughed at, to get told that your ideas, your well-intentioned suggestions, are stuff a 'crackpot' would dream up.

Yeah, there was certainly time for patience, and that time had long passed . . . unless Lax was getting at the patience of waiting for tomorrow.

Though he got the feeling that he wasn't.

He got the feeling he was speaking more in general, and no doubt reciting some old piece of twine his daddy had imparted to him.

One of those old gnomisms.

Bert wondered if Lax expected him to say something back in response. This had been, after all, his idea, and he felt somewhat responsible for what the kid got up to . . . even though he was a forty-something working gnome and more than capable of taking responsibility for himself.

All the same . . .

Bert was about halfway to turning on his side when he heard the *rustle* of leaves.

He spun over.

Looked to the bushes which surrounded the camp.

Which were just about visible in the candlelight.

He saw that their guards had been alerted too.

That the two of them were grasping their rifles, ready to use them.

But then, just like that, with a collective "Yeeeeelp!" from a hidden chorus, gnomes flooded out from the undergrowth and consumed the campsite.

CAUGHT OUT

BERT WAS STRUCK WITH INACTION. He couldn't shift himself from his bunk though there were maybe a dozen gnomes bearing down on him, all of them screaming out at the top of their lungs and swinging their arms about in windmill-like motions as if that was really going to hurt somebody.

Bert only snapped to when he felt Lax grab hold of his wrist and yank him off his bunk, and down onto the ground.

The two of them lay side by side listening to the *patter* of the stampeding gnomes all about them, and the screeching and the calling out among the Juttilian soldiers.

All of a sudden the air was alive with warmth and with smells of herbs and perfumes and colognes, and Bert knew right away that these gnomes, the ones swarming the campsite right now, they were the villagers that'd gone missing all throughout the Dwinns . . . the ones who had seen the invaders coming.

And they had bided their time right till the last moment.

Till the invaders could no longer back out or hide.

While they lay there, half beneath their bunks, Bert got a couple of kicks in the ribs from confused Dwindians, no doubt thinking that he was Juttilian . . . though he guessed he deserved those kicks all the same considering he was *technically* abetting the enemy.

Though, under more civil conditions, he might well have launched into a debate about what that even meant, because, for him, the Council were a far greater enemy than—

A log landed with a *thump* approximately three inches from Bert's head.

He twirled about in panic, caught Lax's eye, and in that moment they decided on the same thing. To scrabble to their feet and to get themselves as far away from the campsite as they possibly could.

Bert heard a couple of gunshots over his shoulder. And as they made it into the hedges, the shots cracked about the place like staccato thunderclaps.

He just kept bombing forwards, Lax alongside him, apparently stuck to his side.

Just as long as they kept together Bert was sure they'd survive.

Another gunshot fired.

It bit into the bark of a tree to Bert's side.

Wood dust puffed up into the air.

Bert breathed some of it in and felt it immediately tickle at the back of his throat. He doubled over as they continued to barrel forwards, near enough coughing his lungs out.

Lax grabbed hold of him again, dragged him on through the hedges.

Bert could hear the *crack* of the twigs as he stomped them. Could feel the branches sticking into his tunic, pinching his skin, and threatening to puncture holes in him. He could still feel that slab of fudge in his breast pocket and, in the confusion, he fished for it and brought it out, somehow offering a piece to Lax who, apparently just as much in shock, took it off him and shoved it into his mouth.

Together, as they rushed on, the two of them chomped on their respective fudge.

As soon as that sugary flavour hit Bert's tongue he found that he could run faster. That he could bound onwards, and make his way faster away from the camp. He could sense Lax keeping speed with him too.

They'd be safe soon.

Just a little further—

Another gunshot.

This time much closer.

Bert wasn't sure which sound came first. The shot or Lax's cry of pain. But he was certain that he saw Lax drop to the ground in the half light from the moon.

Bert trundled on another pace or two then stopped dead, not thinking straight.

Another shot.

Instinctively, he dropped and he heard the rush of air as the bullet fizzled right past his ear. He thought he could feel the heat off it against his skin.

He lay there, on the ground, on the slightly damp grass, alongside Lax.

When Bert sensed that they had been lying there for five

minutes, maybe longer, he reached out for Lax's arm, squeezed it, and said, "You okay?"

Lax was sucking hard at air, clearly in pain.

Bert crawled his way over to his side on his elbows, then, after a quick glance about their surroundings, he propped himself up on his knees and looked Lax over. "Where'd they get you?" he said.

It seemed that the only thing Lax could think to do now was breathe. He certainly didn't seem to have the strength to put whatever he had to say into words. But, in the end, he didn't need to.

Even in just the moonlight, Bert managed to locate where Lax had been shot.

He had a bullet hole in his upper thigh.

Moonlight gleamed off the blood.

Bert looked at it closer. Saw that the bullet had passed right through the surface of Lax's skin, it hadn't penetrated right down to his bone as he'd feared.

Just a flesh wound.

Back over in the direction of the campsite, the callings-out continued, coupled with the occasional *crack* of a rifle going off. He was fairly sure that none of those shots were particularly aimed at anyone. It was too frantic about the camp to take aim at anyone and be sure just who they were. The Dwindians had caught the Juttilians totally off guard, hit them when they least expected it, and they'd succeeded in disrupting everything.

Why, by now Bert was fairly certain that some of the Dwindians would have commandeered rifles, and even if they couldn't figure out how to use them, they would at least stop the Juttilians from using them, and that was almost as good.

He sat there, alongside Lax, and thought about what to do next.

One thing was certain, one thing he'd established, and that was that they'd be much better off not making too many sudden moves out here in the dark.

It seemed that those who still had the rifles were making a point of shooting off into the foliage that surrounded the campsite because that was where they thought yet more Dwindians were lurking.

And, well, they were right in a way.

Because both he and Lax were Dwindians.

Defectors.

But Dwindians all the same.

MORNING LIGHT

B ERT GOT IT into his mind, as he slumped there at Lax's side, that the morning would never come. He could smell that metal-like odour of the blood oozing out of Lax's wound in his thigh, and he knew that he really needed some medical help, and as soon as possible.

But there wouldn't be anything he could do for him till it was full daylight.

And he could be sure that they wouldn't get shot at just out of plain panic.

Bert thought it was almost an illusion when he saw that familiar pinkish glow off on the horizon, that glow of the rising sun that was so familiar to him after the years and years of early starts, of getting up to go and work his mine.

And yet, today, he'd believed it would never come.

When the sun gave enough light for him to make out the basics of his surroundings: to be sure about the trees and hedges which surrounded him, the long grasses, he turned his attention back to Lax, saw that he had his eyes closed and that he was twitching in his sleep.

Yes, that was better for him now.

Better for him to sleep through this thing till Bert could find help.

Bert peered off over the foliage and back in the direction of the camp.

It was a long way off.

A good two, three hundred, or more, paces.

They'd run much further than he'd imagined. That fudge they'd chewed on, why it'd just seemed to push him right along as if he was flying rather than running.

He'd been extremely grateful for that speed last night.

He was even more grateful for it this morning.

Because, as he reminded himself again, the Juttilians might just as easily have had him and Lax executed last night . . . if he'd refused to join with them.

Now he wondered where they stood with the Juttilians, whether they were searching for them, whether they believed that he and Lax had simply taken their chance and run off . . . or maybe they thought that they'd been in on the plan all along, got themselves captured on purpose so that they might sniff out the enemy's weaknesses.

One thing was for certain, Bert could really do without running into that rather stern, stone-faced uniformed gnome again.

Especially if he or anyone close by him was armed.

By his gnome sense, Bert knew it to be around six thirty in the morning, and that was when he decided it was time to wake

Lax up, and to help him to his feet.

Lax grumbled at him, still half asleep despite getting propped up.

Though Bert gave him a couple of light slaps on both cheeks, Lax didn't really seem to respond to him at all.

In the end, Bert had to carry pretty much all of Lax's weight, there was just no way to get through to him at all. He wouldn't respond to anything.

Bert thought about where they'd head for a moment then decided that the only place close by that he knew about, that he would be sure of being able to lug Lax along to, was the campsite they'd fled the night before.

So that was where he carried him along to.

It took the best part of an hour to help Lax through the foliage in his dozed-up state, and to keep him from tripping over any of the many roots that stuck out from the ground.

As the campsite came into sight, Bert saw that it lay in ruins.

That the tents had been reduced to scraps of material by the Dwindians that had stampeded through it.

And there seemed to be really no sign of anybody about the place.

He noticed a few rifles lying about in the tall grasses.

They'd all been damaged in some way.

Had their barrels dented into uselessness with rocks, while others had been snapped in two.

Bert guessed that was *a* response to such firepower, if not a particularly technical one.

Though, he supposed, if he was expecting something technical from Dwindians then he really hadn't been paying much attention for a grand portion of his life.

As he trekked on, now feeling his shoulder muscles about reaching their capacity for fatigue, he noticed their upturned bunks, the ones they'd lain on the night before and stared up at the starry sky. It seemed a long time back now. Almost a different week altogether.

He only realised how soaked the legs of his trousers had got when he turned one of the bunks the right way up and had set Lax down.

He also noticed, as he was feeling his trousers for dampness, that he had a kind of nick in the side of his boot where a bullet had scraped off the top layer of the leather.

He couldn't recall that bullet.

He guessed it must've been while they'd been running away from the campsite.

Listening to the birds twittering in the trees and the leaves rustling in the breeze, Bert wondered just what they were going to do now since they could apparently see nobody around.

It was like nothing at all had happened the night before, as if the battle had just been a bad dream of his, as if all this wreckage that was left over here was nothing more than his imagination.

He held his hand up to shield his eyes from the bright morning sun, and he surveyed the surrounding hills, looking for some clue of someone—alive or dead—who might be about here.

Nothing.

No one.

When he turned back to check on Lax, he saw that he'd gone even paler, paler even than he'd been the day before with his hangover. His lips had take on a kind of purple-blue shade to them and he knew that he needed to get him some help as soon as possible.

But from where?

There was nobody about.

Maybe he should've expected it . . . maybe he should've been paying more attention to his surroundings, but the next thing he knew he felt the blunt tip of a rifle in his back and then that all-too familiar, "Hands up!" from behind him.

Bert did what the gnomic soldier said. He didn't want to get himself shot.

Not while he still had to help Lax pull through.

THERE YOU ARE!!

ARDULL FELT the morning breeze blowing the collar of his jacket up against his neck. He liked that feeling. It brought him alive. Gave him a great freshness.

Where all those Dwindians had come from, Ardull had absolutely no idea.

Well, actually, he did have a feeling that those vacated villages they'd passed through to get here, to this campsite just a little way from Cormersbarn, had something to do with it. That the Dwindians who'd jumped them in the middle of the night had most likely been residents of those places.

Savages, the lot of them, that was how they'd acted.

They hadn't had any weapons beyond sticks and stones.

If it'd been a level-playing field, his gnomes would've made mincemeat of them.

Ardull looked over what remained of his men, less than a hundred all told. That strike from those guerrilla Dwindians had been nothing short of catastrophic for him and the Arrive-and-Occupy plan. Though he'd sent out a few scouts to track down stragglers, or those who'd got disoriented and wandered off, Ardull knew the truth.

That most of his gnomes had deserted him.

That they'd headed off on that long trek back home.

Idiots, every last one of them.

How far did they expect to get without any tents, with only scraps of supplies remaining . . . and, above all *else*, without any solid leadership?

But there was nothing Ardull could do about it now except keep together the gnomes who'd stuck by him during the ambush.

There was one much more pressing issue, an issue that had terrifying consequences all things considered.

His poetry notebook had gone missing.

As his gnomes had scoured the campsite, dug through the collapsed tents and sieved through the remains of the attack, he'd given Jeorge *strict* orders to report to him if he turned up the notebook, and he was to bring it to him straight away.

But Jeorge had found nothing.

And now Ardull's mind was alive with paranoia.

Had the Dwindians found it?

. . . And if they had would they translate his words, publish them?

It didn't bear thinking about . . . so why couldn't Ardull stop thinking about it?

As he surveyed his men's progress through the collapsed campsite, he caught a glance of Jeorge, clutching his rifle, and with a pair of familiar-looking figures.

Was it? . . . Yes, yes it was.

Those two Dwindians they'd captured the day before, the ones who'd agreed to fight by their side as they marched on Cormersbarn.

One of them, Ardull could see from here, was wounded.

Was limping terribly.

Had they tried to escape when those Dwindians had overrun the camp?

More importantly, did they have an idea about where his notebook of verse had got to?

Ardull quickened his step, marched on hard along the soaked earth, feeling the wet grass brush up against his trouser legs. As he drew closer, he felt his heart welling up in his throat in anticipation. He looked them over.

The older, blond one . . . what'd been his name? . . . Flaughterbert, his clothes were stuck with clods of mud and his face was streaked with dirt. His eyes were webbed with bulging, red veins. And he supported his companion, the red-haired one, the one who'd taken a nap in his tent the day before.

Now Ardull saw the wound properly for the first time.

Saw that Flaughterbert had cut away the material of the gnome's trouser leg to get at the wound.

All told they looked like they'd had a rough night.

At least as rough as the night he'd had.

Just behind them he saw Jeorge, looking very pleased with himself, holding that rifle of his, which, rather worryingly, he was pointing right at Ardull's chest . . . *once more*.

Ardull made a subtle gesture for him to lower the rifle, and Jeorge realised just what he'd been doing, restored his rifle to a less dangerous position, and then he stood straight-backed apparently awaiting orders.

"Get this gnome medical help," Ardull said to Jeorge.

Jeorge looked a touch reluctant to leave the recaptured prisoners for a moment, but he soon nodded in response, and obeyed, skittering off to go and find a medic.

Ardull took in the two gnomes, saw how thoroughly *wretched* they looked.

When he happened to glance back over his shoulder, he saw one of his spies, the one who'd acted as an interpreter yesterday. The one with the silver *earring*.

He was on his hands and knees digging about in the wreckage of a tent.

Ardull gave an internal sigh, but knew that there was no other option. So he called for him to come over and to help him out with what he needed to say to the two recaptured prisoners.

He needed assurances.

And he needed them *now*.

HELLO, MY OLD ENEMY

BERT KNEW that he should've felt a touch highly strung to find himself facing off with the uniformed gnome yet again, to find himself at his mercy once more and under such pressing conditions, what with the way that this looked an awful lot like they'd attempted a sneaky escape only to be apprehended. Only for Lax to get himself shot.

The jumpered gnome from the day before, the one with the silver earring, sprung up at his superior's side. He listened to what his superior had to say, and then turned to Bert and Lax, "Do not worry, there is medical help on its way."

Bert managed a faint nod. He really felt like he had no more energy left about him, felt like he was just about as forceful, and of as much use as, a damp blanket right now.

Though Lax wasn't exactly a weighty fellow, he certainly wasn't light as a feather by any means, and he'd spent most of the morning keeping him upright.

The uniformed gnome seemed to realise this and he nodded for the jumpered gnome / translator, to go over and give a little help.

The jumpered gnome hesitated for a second, apparently on the brink of admitting out loud to his boss that he thought this task beneath him.

But he did it in the end.

While the jumpered gnome didn't take all the weight off Bert, he did take a good amount of Lax's left shoulder, and Bert felt like he could much better manage now.

The uniformed gnome muttered off something else and the jumpered gnome said, "He wants to know what happened—why you ran away."

Bert shook his head, felt his stomach give an inelegant *growl* of hunger, then said, "We didn't run away. We were just as scared as you lot were. We didn't want to get ourselves stomped on, or worse."

The jumpered gnome translated and the uniformed gnome took this piece of information with pursed lips.

The reply came quickly from the uniformed gnome, and Bert guessed that this was a matter of some importance.

The jumpered gnome said, "He wants to know if you might have seen a notebook anywhere about the campsite." He paused a moment, slipped a glance to his superior, and then looked back to Bert and Lax, now using his hands to gesture. "It's about this big," the jumpered gnome said, "and it has lots of writing in it."

Bert stretched his mind. Thought back to the day before. To when they'd been in the uniformed officer's tent and he'd seen that notebook on the floor. For some reason, instead of saying that he didn't know, he replied to the jumpered gnome saying, "With poetry in it?"

A quick exchange between the uniformed gnome and the jumpered gnome, and then, "Yes. Yes, that's the one. It had some poetry in it."

For some reason this tickled Bert as much today as it had the day before. Just that whole absurdity of a general scrawling out his soul onto a bunch of pages. What was he trying to pull? Was he trying to show off his sensitive side?

Bert found himself beginning to smile but then stopped himself, realising that he was just being a *touch* mean. After all, he really knew nothing at all about the uniformed gnome, none of his background, nothing.

And, considering how little he knew of the Juttilians, for all he knew they might've had enforced conscription: supported slave armies.

And though the uniformed officer here was apparently good at his job, good at this whole Arrive-and-Occupy thing of his, he might have just been nothing more than a victim of circumstance.

So Bert kept the belly laughs tucked away for later on.

Finally, Bert shook his head to confirm that he hadn't run across the notebook with the poetry all scrawled within it.

But there was something else too, because the uniformed officer didn't take the opportunity of Bert saying that he knew nothing of the notebook to stalk away in a huff.

No, the uniformed officer's face went greyer still and his words toppled out from between his lips like cement slabs rubbing up against each other.

The jumpered officer translated, "You do realise the predicament that this leaves us in—*us* as allies, that now it shall be impossible for the Arrive-and-Occupy operation to proceed, that it will not be possible to overthrow this Council you so disapprove of."

"Why's that?" Bert said.

With no need to consult the uniformed gnome, the jumpered gnome replied, "Because we lost a great number of our gnomes last night—they deserted."

He gestured about him with his hands, to those who remained, all of them scratching about the remains of the deflated tents, others among them picking at the beaten-up rifles as if they might get them to shoot again if they just worked hard at it.

The jumpered gnome continued, "We will be forced to retreat also."

AW

BERT FELT HIS STOMACH KNOT. He knew that he should've felt glad. That these enemy, *invading*, forces were leaving the Domain, that they'd head away from their lands, go back to their own Domain.

At the same time, though, he knew that these gnomes promised true change, they promised the change that he had strived for, in one form or another, for his entire life.

If he let them go now then it would only be to condemn future generations of Dwindians to lifetimes of incompetent rule . . . his children—if he did eventually find that lady gnome— would most likely never leave the village they were born into, there would be no promise of a *real* transportation infrastructure, however basic.

Any gnome who wanted to get about would have to use their own two feet.

And he hadn't even got started on defence, because if another Domain decided that they wanted to step in and invade the Dwinns they could do so quite easily.

Bert couldn't help but think to himself that this invasion by the Juttilians was not the end of the matter, he thought that word would spread extremely quickly.

There would be other Domains who thought that they could take hold of the Dwinns if they only exerted a very minimum of military force.

And they might not be quite as well-intentioned as he was sure the Juttilians were . . . as he'd come to believe over the past twenty-four hours, sort of in incarceration.

When Bert snapped to, he saw that a medic gnome was padding up to them. He had a snow-white beard which matched the white armband he wore on the upper arm of his camos.

With the jumpered gnome's help, Bert laid Lax down on a collapsed tent cloth and then took a few steps away to give the medic some room.

With Lax and the medic occupied, it left the jumpered gnome, the uniformed gnome, and Bert just standing about and looking on.

Bert knew that he had to think of something—that he had to come up with some sort of a plan or else the Dwinns, their home, would find itself overrun by foreign invaders.

And he was certain that there wasn't going to be any sort of change going about the process democratically.

No, it was much too late for that now.

Now he had to take the matter into his own hands, and use physical force if necessary.

Bert noticed the uniformed gnome barking off orders at his

men, and Bert watched on as the gnomes all gathered up the remains of the campsite, pawing the tent cloth into ragged little packages while stockpiling the knackered rifles.

If only . . . if only he could . . . could he really?

. . . No, it was a ridiculous proposition.

Better for him just to forget the whole thing.

If he was lucky, the foreign invaders, when they eventually *did* come, would leave him in peace in his mansion, and with his mining operation.

His *extremely* lucrative mining operation.

Yeah, right.

His mind kept spinning back onto that one wild, utterly hair-brained idea, but no matter what he did, he couldn't quite seem to get himself shot of the notion.

He tried to remind himself that the time for dreaming—the time for longing for change—had passed a long while back, and now he had to just content himself with the way things were going to be.

It was folly to do anything else.

And yet . . . this time he gave himself a hearty slap on the side of his head in an attempt to get his brain to stop thinking about it.

The pain burrowed through his skin and into his skull where it tingled.

Say what you like about hitting yourself in the head, but sometimes it's the only way of getting the thoughts to stop coming.

His mind blanked out . . . and then it came back to him.

He looked to the uniformed gnome, viewed him in profile,

and guessed that it was worth a go, that the uniformed gnome would surely hear him out, if only to laugh at him afterwards.

Perhaps they all needed a little laughter right about now.

And so, with a final glance down to the medic, still patching up Lax's thigh, he turned to the uniformed gnome and told him of his plan.

REALLY?

A RDULL had to keep his mind focussed on the lips of his spy-turned-interpreter as he spoke, but still he couldn't quite decide if what he was hearing was really exactly as this Flaughterbert gnome put it.

Oh, he could hear Flaughterbert jabbering away, but he really had no hope of understanding more than the odd phrase or word here and there. Truth be told, his ineptitude in foreign languages had seen off, once and for all, that pipedream he'd nursed so long ago, that dream of entering into a diplomatic position—of working as an ambassador to this Domain, or that Domain.

It really would've been a quite perfect career for him.

But here he was, right now, a general no less.

That was a decent consolation prize, he supposed.

The upshot of what Flaughterbert told him through the interpreter was that Flaughterbert planned on going to the gnomes who had fled the villages in an attempt to convince them to join forces with what remained of Ardull's rag-tag Arrive-and-Occupy troop.

To be honest, Ardull couldn't quite see the idea getting off the ground, but he listened in all the same. It seemed, after all, that Flaughterbert was just trying to help out.

And he did appear genuinely interested in getting shot of the Gnomish Council of the Dwinns, and that, when all was said and done, was nicely inline with his own ambitions.

When his interpreter had told him everything he needed to know, everything of use that'd flopped out from Flaughterbert's gums, Ardull turned out and looked to the landscape surrounding.

A beautiful day, all blue skies and sun-streamed clouds. He could hear the *chatter* of insects in the long grasses and the twitter of birds in the trees. When he breathed in, he caught that utterly *fresh* scent of nature—unadulterated and consistently new. He felt his veins throbbing just a little now, crying out for more yaltas leaves though there would be none for him to ingest. His mouth was still dry and tasteless, like he had a coating of ash inside his cheeks.

He had wanted to stay here, had *dreamed* of staying here.

It'd be such an idyllic life, so different from the grind of his very urban Juttle . . . though he supposed that he did love the place also, but in a very different way.

No, all things considered, he would've sent for his wife and children the day after he'd taken hold of Cormersbarn, and once they'd arrived he would've gone and picked out the most pleasant little cottage that he could come across—perhaps somewhere out in the depths of the Domain, with a lake, where he could lie beside the lapping waters and just scrawl out his poetry till the sun set everyday.

He could hardly believe that the cost of living in the Dwinns was all that dear.

And he had a decent pension to fall back on for whenever he decided to call time on his military career, which he had all intention of doing so.

Life would've been grand and simple indeed.

But he had failed, and that would be the legacy that would haunt him now, if he returned home to his superiors and gave them his report, told them just how it had happened.

Oh, there would be court-martials, for sure, and the official explanation would no doubt praise his leadership skills, his contribution to the operation, but Ardull, and the rest, would all the know the truth, would know that the operation *had* been a failure.

Ardull would leave his post, would *resign*, a failure.

And, though Ardull wished there might be another way, he really saw no other path.

At least he would have more time for his poetry now, though it seemed a great pity that he would lose the verse he'd scrawled down in the course of the operation.

But back to this proposal of Flaughterbert's . . . could it be worth a shot?

What was the worst thing that could come about if it all went awry?

They would go to the gnomes, to those gnomes they'd driven out of their own homes, and into hiding, into forming this guerrilla band, and they'd lay out all the claims in as best a fashion that they could manage.

And then the gnomes, if they decided not to kill them out of hand, would consider the proposal and make a decision based on that.

It would require great trust to be placed in Flaughterbert's hands.

Would require Flaughterbert to be a greatly convincing gnome.

But what was the alternative?

And so, with his mind made up, Ardull turned on Flaughterbert and gave a stiff, slightly apprehensive, nod of his head.

Now they'd see if anything could be salvaged from this.

BACK IN ACTION

B ERT COULD HEAR his heart drumming in his ears, and could feel his muscles all stiffening up. They'd trekked on through the night, using one of the uniformed gnome's tracking specialists.

The uniformed gnome had turned out to be called General Ardull, or simply Ardull, as he'd insisted, despite Bert being technically under his command.

As Bert trudged along through the freezing cold air, hugging himself for warmth and glad for the wad of fudge he had to munch on, he observed the tracker and decided that tracking pretty much constituted staying fairly low to the ground and staring at the mud.

But Bert wasn't complaining, after all, he wasn't much in his element here, and he had no reason not to trust in the competence of Ardull's gnomes after the great job they'd done of patching up Lax. And along with the fact that he'd placed all his trust in Ardull's Arrive-and-Occupy operation bringing forth Domain-wide changes to the Dwinns.

He *banked* on Ardull having a competent operation behind him.

When Bert breathed in, it was like he was breathing icicles, direct down his throat and into his lungs where they'd tingle about his chest for a while, giving him that drowsy, heavy-headed feeling that he'd get before a cold would catch him in its grip.

As he beat on along the trail, he glanced back over his shoulder, saw Lax still limping along with the aid of a couple of Ardull's men, keeping him propped between the two of them. They'd considered leaving him behind but Ardull had stated that it'd be much better for them all to stay together rather than risk ambush yet again.

After all, the guerrilla gnomes had caught them flat-footed once and so Ardull was most likely determined not to let it happen again.

Bert steadied his shoulders and kept pace with the military gnomes. It was funny, before he'd embarked on this quest he'd always considered himself to be in pretty good shape for a gnome of his age . . . but, really, he was nothing on these Juttilians who, he now realised, had been through hell and back just to get to this point.

As he wandered onwards, he heard the gentle *squidge* of boots behind him as they pressed on through the thick mud throughout this glade. He glanced to his side and saw General Ardull there, along with the jumpered gnome, the interpreter, skipping about every three steps to keep time with his superior.

Ardull maintained his stony face and Bert observed those

deep, dark circles beneath his eyes, saw the face that looked a little like it hadn't slept properly in days.

But, then again, that probably followed what with him being a general of this whole operation, meticulously planning an attack on a town only to have a solid nine-tenths of his troop desert him.

Not knowing sufficient Juttilian to sprout anything resembling small talk, Bert just gave him a "Hello," in his own language, which the interpreter duly translated . . . perhaps unnecessarily given the searing glare he got off Ardull for his trouble.

Ardull looked off along the soldiers, up to the front of the group, and Bert followed his gaze, felt a tightness in his chest as he wondered just how they were getting on.

He didn't have too long to wait.

Ardull drawled out something in Juttilian and the jumpered gnome translated.

"He says," the jumpered gnome began, "that the tracker believes we are closing on the location of the guerrilla gnomes."

"Oh," Bert said, "and how does he know that?"

The jumpered gnome shrugged. "More footprints about here. All the signs point to them having a base somewhere about this place. This is their camp."

"And which direction do you think they're based?"

Again, the jumpered gnome shrugged. "Well, to be honest, we've just been going in circles for the last few hours . . . not much else for us to do about it—at least that's what the tracker says."

Bert nodded to him, and then looked off to Ardull who kept up that same thousand-yard stare, looking off to the front of the troops, as if locked onto something important that Bert just didn't have a chance of seeing because he wasn't much more than a country bumpkin at heart. At least that was how Bert thought Ardull saw him.

Then again, Bert thought he could read something in Ardull's manner, the way that he kept chewing with his jaw, that way Bert got whenever he didn't have any fudge to wodge into his mouth. Could he be a fudge fanatic like Bert?

He thought that, really, there was nothing to lose, so he dug into the inside pocket of his tunic, broke off a piece from his flat square of fudge and offered it to Ardull.

Ardull frowned for a moment, all those wrinkles appearing in his forehead, then he took the offered fudge from Bert, sniffed at it, and then looked at him. "What is this?" he said through his interpreter.

"Well it's not poison," Bert said, "so don't worry about that."

There was a slight glimmer in Ardull's eye that told Bert that, perhaps, he hadn't picked the best time to crack a joke . . . that they weren't quite *that* grounded in their friendship to be throwing matters such as murder about too freely.

But, against all odds, Ardull cracked a wry smile, then bit off a corner of the fudge. He chomped away at it, and Bert observed the rosiness, even visible in the moonlight, return to Ardull's cheeks. And he was almost certain that he could see those dark circles receding from beneath his eyes like the disappearance of shadows at midday.

Ardull popped the rest of the fudge in his mouth, and chewed on it pensively.

Bert couldn't help smiling himself. He knew that, if Ardull hadn't been a fudge fanatic before this moment, he was one now.

And whatever it was that had plagued him, whatever it was that was making his jaw chomp like that, it was on the way to being exorcised for good.

"Hmm," Ardull said, his mouth full of fudge. "Mmm."

Bert took those as sounds of contentment, and they all trekked on together in glad silence. Just the sounds of their gentle push forth through the long grasses and muddy soil.

They'd only been going another five, maybe ten minutes, when Bert heard a *rustle* off in the bushes to his left. So too, it seemed, had the tracker, who halted, stood stock still and stared off in the direction of the sound.

The whole group of soldiers came to a halt, and they all looked off to that same spot.

Almost as soon as they'd come to a stop, Bert heard another sound off to their right. Another *rustle*. And then behind. And then up front.

A few torches flamed into life, all about them.

And, just like that, they were surrounded.

Surrounded by the guerrilla gnomes.

WELL, THAT'S ONE WAY TO DO IT

A S BERT'S eyes grew accustomed to the flickering flames of the torches, he took in the gnomes that surrounded them. There must've been well over a thousand of them, and they all carried rocks or branches or rifles—some of them turned the wrong way around.

No one said anything for a long time, and it was only with a slight "Oh!" that he watched the interpreter with the silver earring being poked away from the main group to apparently interface with the guerrilla gnomes that surrounded them.

Bert could feel his heart ticking by slowly, could feel it tickling at his tonsils, and he knew that, right now, he was in a *very* precarious position. Here he was, a Dwindian gnome consorting with the enemy.

Lax, too, was in great danger.

The interpreter asked to speak with the leader of the group, and an elderly gnome, which was to say a gnome who was a few years older than Bert, stepped out from between the parting line of gnomes.

He had a golden beard and fierce eyebrows. He wore a purple stocking cap the tail of which hung down at his chest. The tail had a fluffy cotton bobble on it too, which kind of worked against the mean expression and generally *angered* demeanour the gnome was trying to strike.

But Bert couldn't fault him for trying.

"Whatcha doin'?" the golden-bearded gnome said. "Thinkin' a beatin' a retreat, or wha'?"

Bert could hear that the gnome had a thick accent, and he wondered if he was a farmer or something. He'd often heard farmers speak like that. But chances were that, like most of the population of the Dwinns, he was a scammer.

Just a well-respected one, that was all.

Bert decided that now was as good a time as any for him to make his contribution to this stupid idea of his, so he took a step forwards, and decided to take his own life into his hands by speaking . . . and thus revealing to the gnomes who surrounded them that he was, without doubt, a Dwindian just like they were.

A *traitor*.

"Look," Bert said, starting somewhat unconvincingly with that crutch word he seemed incapable of being able to let go, "these men, these *Juttilians*, it's true that they've come here to take over—to take over the Dwinns . . ."

This remark was greeted with much grumbling among the gnomes and, Bert noticed, more than one fist clenched a little tighter about branch or rock or unconvincingly-held rifle.

Bert continued all the same, "But you must understand that the way things are, the way things have always been in the

Dwinns, that they've got to change. The Council, that group of gnomes who have kept us as backward gnomes all our lives—kept our taxes for . . . goodness knows what, while they sit about there in the Seat and do *nothing*."

Someone coughed among the guerrilla gnomes and Bert flinched, convinced that this might well be a signal for them to start into the soldiers. Because he was certain that if the gnomes decided they wanted to fight against them then they'd easily overthrow the lot of them, even despite the few rifles that Ardull's gnomes still had in their possession.

Bert felt the weight of the gnomes' gaze on him, not just of the guerrilla gnomes, but of Ardull and his gnomes too. Everyone was depending on him, waiting to see just what he had to say before deciding whether or not a physical conflict would be necessary here.

"We have nothing here," Bert continued, "in the Dwinns we live our lives in the villages where we're born—there's no transport between villages, no horse-drawn carts for us to be able to move produce about the Domain more easily, nor is there any stable education, no solid, Domain-wide syllabus for us to base our cultural growth upon. Our children simply run wild and learn our old habits, grow up with dishonesty and believe that's not the most noble way, but the *only* way."

He drew a profound breath, glanced about him expecting a missile of some description to be heading his way any second now . . . and quite hoping that he'd have the opportunity to duck, though he wouldn't bet on it.

"And our defence," he went on, hoping that they'd start to see sense now, and that they'd realise that there was only one way forward, "we have nothing. No armed forces. No means for us to keep up the control of our frontiers." He glanced over Ardull's men, threw his arm out behind him to indicate them. "Why, they got their way into the Domain without so much as a bruise because our only strategy was to hide away like cowards. To disperse, to run off. We must arm ourselves or we'll find ourselves overrun with other gnomes, from *other* Domains, don't think that this all ends when the Juttilians here pass out of our lands."

He could hear mumbling about between the guerrilla gnomes now, and he hoped that he was getting through to *one* gnome at least. It was all about getting through to *one* person, because that gnome could then potentially convince another gnome—and then another, and then another.

Now it was time for those words he'd spent a good portion of the march over here thumbing over in his mind. He had to get them out just right, otherwise they might well find themselves torn to pieces for his trouble.

"Now's the time," he continued, "if we want to take back our Domain, if we want to bring about a true change in our lives, and the way that we live, then the only solution is for us to stand up alongside the Juttilians and aid them in overthrowing the Council, and have them instate another."

He turned his attention to the golden-bearded gnome, the leader of the bunch, and saw that he was curling his beard about his fingers.

He *prayed* that he was getting through to some of them.

That *someone* was taking all this in.

At least if they gave the order to kill them now, to reject them, then later *one* gnome among these guerrilla gnomes would think about what it was that Bert had said, and they would see some sort of reason in it.

That was all that Bert could hope for now.

And that would be enough of a legacy for him.

It seemed everyone's eyes were fixed on the golden-bearded gnome, his fingers still buried in his beard, and his eyes sifting the air before his crooked, bony nose.

He tilted his head back, met Bert's eyes, and then gave him a stiff, regretful nod. "We shall spare you for the night," he said, and then looked back to the gnomes who surrounded him, nodded to a few of them and they swarmed into the soldiers, into Ardull's men, relieved them of their arms, and tied up their hands with thick twine.

They tied both Bert and Lax's hands too, and why wouldn't they?

After all, they were traitors.

HQ

I RONICALLY, though Bert spent a good proportion of his time underground at his mine, he really wasn't much of a fan of being underground.

And that, as it turned out, was where the guerrilla gnomes were hiding out.

As he trudged along at the front of the group, a pair of gnomes flanking him, he breathed in that familiar smell of soil and cursed not having shoved in another wad of fudge before they'd tied his hands behind his back. He'd just have to imagine that sugary taste, those rich and almost fruity notes of his favourite food.

It was cool too down here, that kind of muddy cold that ran about underground. And the muddy walls seemed to absorb all sound of their footsteps as they proceeded downwards, further into the gloom of the hole, leaving the moonlight behind once and for all.

As he walked along, he noticed the golden-bearded gnome strut up alongside him, a slight smirk marking his lips. His fingers still fondling his beard. "You know," he said, "we dug this place all out in a day or so, not bad, eh?"

Bert glanced about him, having to squint a little in the torch-light. Funny that he'd had such great night vision before, been great at seeing down in even the darkest of the underground places, but he guessed that he'd lost a little of that ability seeing as he'd spent so much time up on the surface, in sunlight.

Still, he guessed he'd get back his night vision soon enough.

And then he'd be killed.

He *could* make out the teeth marks, though. The way that the gnomes had dug their headquarters out with their mouths—just as he'd dug out his mine with his teeth, just as he *mined* with his teeth.

He wondered if the Dwindian gnomes had learned anything from this experience—if they realised that, when they put their minds—and mouths—to it they could quite easily start up their own mining operations.

Though Bert had no intention of letting any other gnomes in on the racket that was independent mining, he wondered if they'd actually uncovered anything of value that they might sell and come to that conclusion themselves.

Time would tell, he guessed.

They snaked along, down the dirt slope, and a large drop sprung up on Bert's right side. Perhaps it was a good thing that his eyes were still adapting to the darkness. He could only just about make out that the space to his right was of a different consistency to the wall on his left. But he couldn't make out the depths all laid out below.

The slope began to level out and Bert got the feeling that they were nearing their location. Indeed, as they got themselves down to the base of the slope, the glow of torchlight greeted them, along with a pair of gnomes, both of them gripping rifles that looked like they'd seen better days . . . and both of them held the rifles vertically but with the butt pointing to the ceiling.

The Dwinns *really* did need that defence budget.

And fast.

The golden-bearded gnome nodded to the gnomes with rifles and they stepped aside, allowing access to the doorway between them, which, Bert was glad to notice, had another pair of torches gleaming out from within.

Bert chanced a glance over his shoulder, back at the others who were now prisoners of the guerrilla gnomes. Among their numbers, he picked out Ardull's face and then Lax's. Every gnome among them had two guerrilla gnomes accompanying them. That, Bert supposed, was the beauty of outnumbering your enemy.

The golden-bearded gnome signalled for Bert's escorts to bring him along behind him, through the doorway, and Bert found himself confronted with a much larger area than he'd first anticipated.

Actually, to be honest, he was quite impressed.

It was a kind of underground amphitheatre, all dug out of the mud here, and all arranged in a half moon of various steps leading down to the stage at the base of it. He guessed that all thousand or so of the guerrilla gnomes could quite comfortably be seated along these steps to listen to whatever wisdom the golden-bearded gnome had to impart.

The golden-bearded gnome led Bert all the way down those

dug-out steps, and deeper into the headquarters of the guerrilla gnomes. Bert found it a mite tricky to keep his balance as he headed on down those steps. He wasn't all that used to having his hands bound and found that, actually, it *did* affect his centre of gravity somewhat.

When they got down to the stage of the amphitheatre, the golden-bearded gnome brought the procession to a halt, and he watched on as the rest of Bert's allies, the Juttilians, were brought up onto the stage, one by one, all their hands still bound.

Bert found himself standing beside Ardull and Lax, along with the jumpered gnome—the translator—close by, and, he also noted, the gnomic soldier who'd caught them a pair of times, and who he'd since found out was called Jeorge.

He watched on as the guerrilla gnomes, some of them brandishing newly acquired rifles from the capture of the Juttilians, filed orderly into the rows of the mud steps and then sat themselves down, chattering amongst themselves, as if they were about to witness some sort of a spectacle, a form of entertainment, or something like it.

The golden-bearded gnome assumed his position at the centre of the stage. He asked for quiet in the hall, and the rest of the guerrilla gnomes went silent.

Bert was a touch surprised that they respected him so readily, given the Dwindian gnomes' capacity for disobeying any form of moral or *actual* code of ethics.

But Bert guessed that he'd learned something new just about every day of this quest of his.

And so, with the newly quietened hall, the golden-bearded gnome spoke.

"Friends, it has come time for us to decide on that which our brother, Flaughterbert Mhyresgnome, has presented us."

Bert thought getting called a 'brother' was a somewhat promising sign, though he wasn't about to count his chickens just yet.

The golden-bearded gnome continued, "The offer is a clear one, and one which I think there really is no reason to spend too much time discussing. As you heard, out there, on the plains, Flaughterbert wishes that we join with him and this band of Juttilian gnomes in overthrowing the Council of Cormersbarn so that we might instate a more *suitable* form of government." He paused, glanced about the faces of the gnomes all sat there then added, "Are there any questions before we hold the vote?"

Bert looked about the gnomes, saw them all turn to their neighbours and begin busy conversations, he overheard some snatches of what was said, of them speaking about their children, and their futures, and Bert just dared to hope, dared to feel that warmth at the pit of his gut burning away there, promising him *something* now.

A *solution* at last.

No one raised their hands to ask a question and so the golden-bearded gnome brought them all back down to silence, had them all listen to his words as he called for the vote.

A simple 'for' or 'against.'

Easy.

Much easier, Bert thought a touch bitterly, than the matter really deserved.

This *was* a fairly multi-levelled proposal, after all.

But he did have to acknowledge that it came down, in the end, to whether or not they wished to abet the enemy, whether they would shrug off their training, their patriotism and see what was the best for them, and their Domain.

Bert held his breath, watched the hands flurry upwards into the air, and all his hopes and dreams be shot down right before his eyes.

A landslide.

Far more than three quarters of the room voted against joining with them, and launching a strike on Cormersbarn.

This was it.

The end.

All that he feared had come to pass now.

When the golden-bearded gnome turned around now, his features were darkened, and Bert saw a new sharpness, a new fearlessness in his eyes.

And he guessed that he might have underestimated this band of gnomes, and the strength of their organisation.

"Take the prisoners away," the golden-bearded gnome said, without emotion in his voice.

WHAT?

ARDULL got most of what was going on through the medium of his interpreter who hardly had time to bark out those final lines to him as the golden-bearded gnome turned around and, with those proud lips of his, declared that they should be taken away.

That they were prisoners.

Ardull managed to get off a fiery glance in Flaughterbert's direction but he knew, in his heart of hearts, that this was just as much his fault for having clutched at straws, needing to save face and to have one final victory before retirement.

And now he'd cost himself and his most loyal of gnomes their lives.

The only real consolation in this whole matter was the fudge, as Bert had called it, which he still had nestling at the back of his mouth. That was the one thing that had successfully taken his mind off the lack of yaltas leaves, and which he could feel giving him warm energy flowing right to the base of his gut.

He did nothing to oppose the gnomes leading him and his gnomes away. There was nothing that he *could* do. They had them outnumbered at least ten to one, if not more, and once again he cursed all those gnomes who'd taken the opportunity to desert when these Dwindians had overrun the campsite.

If only his gnomes had pulled together, if only they hadn't been cowards, then they might not have found themselves in this predicament right now.

The escort gnomes led them off down a narrow—but extremely well-dug—secondary tunnel leading away from that stage-like area where they'd cast the vote.

Ardull had always been a great admirer of those gnomes who had the talent for digging because he had never been much good at it. Indeed, it wasn't much of a cultivated skill amongst Juttil-ians who were, on the whole, surface-dwelling gnomes.

Yes, the lines from the tooth marks which scored the walls all about the tunnel were really quite sublime, even Ardull could admire that. Funny to think that now, as he and his gnomes were marched into what would surely be their final dwelling place before their execution, that he should wonder to himself about what could have been if he'd only taken a different path, really made a go at being a craftsgnome.

But all he found himself longing for now was his notebook of poetry, so that he might finish his verse before he died.

Within his chest, he felt a warmth and he found himself turning to Jeorge, led by his own pair of escort gnomes, who seemed to read his mind because he looked off to the interpreter gnome and rattled off the command.

Ardull watched on, his heart beating hard, as the interpreter tried to make himself understood to the guards, tried to make what Ardull wanted understood.

The two escort gnomes exchanged glances and seemed a little confused about what they should say . . . or was that what they *could* say?

Ardull felt his chest tightening. If they really did know anything about his notebook, and his poetry scrawled within, then it would be an act of utmost meanness for them to keep the information from him, *him* a condemned gnome.

But Ardull watched on as the escort gnomes jabbered away to one another in Dwindish, and then one of them passed the message on back along the long line of prisoners.

Ardull heard the same chattered word pass along the line, the line that he supposed meant 'notebook' or something like it.

He watched the line of mutterings turn the corner and slip out of sight.

He turned back to face the direction they were travelling in, and saw the large chamber—again, *beautifully* dug out from the ground—that awaited them up ahead.

Would they just kill them here?

Bash their brains in with rocks, or commit some other savage act to end their lives?

Whatever the means, it would have the same result.

For a final time, before he was jabbed in the back with what felt like a rock, shoved on into the chamber along with the rest of his men, he glanced over his shoulder.

But he could see no sign of his notebook being brought forth.

No sign that it had been tracked down.

At least not yet.

Ardull stood with Jeorge on one side and his interpreter on the other. He couldn't help but fix his glare on his interpreter's earring.

To think that he would die beside a gnome with an earring . . . a fully grown *gnome*, no less. This, certainly, was not how he had hoped the annals of history would remember him.

A GLIMMER OF HOPE

B ERT WAS CRAMMED IN with the rest of them, the rest of Ardull's gnomes, into a chamber carved out of the muddy underground. He could feel the gnomes all about him bustling to get just a little space in this quite cosy space.

There was no door to the chamber, only a space, but it was manned by a pair of guerrilla gnomes, each of them brandishing a rifle . . . still turned the wrong way up, but probably just as deadly in those inexpert hands.

He looked about him, looked for some kind of a way out of here.

A glimmer of hope.

But he found nothing at all.

He noticed Lax alongside him.

Lax's complexion had turned a dark purple, and his eyelids drooped down. Bert guessed that he was in need of a good rest. Since his injury he'd really not had a chance to relax. He had had to march along with everyone else, albeit with a pair of gnomes to help him along the way.

Bert reached out and supported Lax, knowing that there was no room for him to lie down, no way for him to spread himself and his wounded thigh out. This was the best he was going to get in the way of a rest.

"You okay?" Bert said, trying to make himself sound as sympathetic as possible . . . not particularly easy given their current predicament, what with them all being on the brink of being killed, or whatever.

"Mm," Lax replied.

Bert gave Lax just a little jig, trying to wake him up a little, snap him out of the pain-inflicted daze that he'd descended into. He wondered if Ardull and his gnomes might have some kind of medicine for Lax to take—something to take the edge off his pain.

"You know," Bert said, "this was the best we could do, and it's really been great having you along for the ride. I'm glad that you stuck by me through all this, you've really been a true friend."

"Mm," Lax said, his eyelids drooping down yet further and leaning more of his, not insignificant, weight onto Bert.

Bert couldn't think of anything more to say . . . nothing reassuring in any case, so, together, they stood there, and Bert watched as the gnomes with the rifles kept an eye on them all. He wondered what would happen to them now. The golden-bearded gnome had at least promised them that they'd live the night . . . but did that just mean that tomorrow they would all be executed first thing?

Could he trust the golden-bearded gnome to tell the truth, not to have them all killed, right here, in this chamber?

Thinking just seemed to fry Bert's brains, so he tried to stop himself getting bogged down in it all . . . and he failed quite rapidly.

Seeing as he couldn't stop his thinking, he decided to turn his mind to something somewhat more useful, to just how he might get himself and Lax, at least, out of this mess.

He glanced out across the gnomes, all those Juttilians.

They looked tired and weary and drawn from all the constant movement.

It was almost like they would be glad to see an end to all this —for them to have some sort of a conclusion to this miserable failure of an operation.

Bert felt his heart squeeze in his chest. If there was one thing that he abhorred above all else it was the maltreatment of gnome upon gnome. There was no reason for it other than cruelty and he was determined that he would not let them down just like this.

He *had* to think of something to get them all out, to get them all free.

And then, right there, like that, it struck him.

A bolt out of the blue . . . or well, more like the mulchy-brown . . .

JUST THE THING!

W ITH HIS MIND now running a mile a minute, Bert turned to Lax, gave him a shake that, in retrospect, was perhaps a touch too hard for a gnome still overcoming a wound like he had. But he shook him hard all the same because he simply couldn't contain himself.

"Your family!" Bert said through gritted teeth as if the gnomes on the door might overhear him and move quickly to snuff out this masterstroke.

They didn't, and they didn't.

"Wha . . . ?" Lax said, still struck by his daze.

"You said, your village—your *gnomes*, they all went missing, didn't they? So don't you think they'll be about here somewhere? Shouldn't they be down here with the rest of these escaped gnomes?"

Lax looked eminently puzzled, as if he was staring into a

thick mist and trying to make out the shape of something or other.

"Can't you *see*?" Bert said, feeling himself getting more and more wound up, driven more and more manic by this idea.

Lax blinked a few times. Swallowed. And then looked to Bert with a shaky gaze.

"Come on," Bert said, "it's worth a go, isn't it?"

Lax gave him a vague nod and Bert took that as an emphatic "Yes," and dragged him off through the gnomes and towards the guards at the door—the ones with the upturned rifles.

Bert looked the gnomes over and garnished right away that these two particular gnomes had almost certainly been chosen for their height and weight, which was to say that the two of them were at least a head and shoulders taller than Bert, and maybe twice as wide.

And those rifles *really* didn't look any less threatening for being turned the wrong-side up in their grasp.

"Uh," Bert started, a touch unconvincingly, "my friend here, he's uh—"

"Shu' up traitor!" one of the gnomes said, bringing his rifle up in his hands and pointing the butt right at the tip of Bert's nose.

"I'd, um," Bert said, "be a little careful with that, if I were you, I mean—"

"Shu' up, and go back over there!" his companion pitched in.

Bert tried his best to smile but it sort of just shrivelled up and died on his lips before it really got any sort of chance to shine. He looked from one gnome to the next, trying to work out just how both of them had got their noses to look so squashed.

He guessed that there was, most likely, a quite interesting, and possibly extremely *violent* story behind that.

"Look," Bert said, determined this time not to be cut off by a pair of meatheads, "my friend here, he's got family among you— gnomes that he knows."

The gnome pointing the butt of the rifle at Bert's chest . . . and the barrel of the rifle at his own chest, looked to Lax who was resting up against Bert's shoulder. Then he looked back to Bert, furrowing his brow and obviously trying to fathom just what sort of a trick he was getting played on him here.

"Couldn't we, uh, *speak* with your superior?" Bert said.

The two gnomes exchanged glances, muttered a word between them, and then the gnome with the rifle said, bluntly, "No."

"Ah," Bert said, his eyes moving from one to the other, and trying to see just how the way forward from this situation would go.

He looked beyond the two massive gnomes and out into the corridor behind them, all lit up with torchlight. He was sort of vaguely wishing that someone who looked just like Lax would wander past and he'd be able to call out to them, have them recognise Lax and have an emotional reunion ensue . . . but, of course, that didn't happen, for the same reason that the majority of inhabitants of the Dwinns, no matter how much they wished for it, never won the lottery.

Mostly because they didn't buy a ticket, but that was sort of beside the point.

He turned his attention back to the gnomes before him trying to see some way that he might be able to get past them. He decided to lean back on what had got them all into such trouble in the first place. "Uh," Bert said, "have either of you two ever thought of joining the army?"

A pair of furrowed brows greeted that then the one with the rifle butt still pointed at Bert's chest, and apparently the more vocal of the two, said, "Wha's tha'?"

Bert resisted the urge to give these two one of his broadest, smuggest smirks, and instead met both of their eyes, one by one, and said, "Well, it's sort of an organisation—a *fighting* organisation," he put in, remembering his audience, "and their duty is to protect the Domain, to see off threats from evildoers, from other gnomes who want to invade."

"Like this lot?" the gnome said.

"Hmm," Bert said, "oh yes, that's right, just like this lot— now think about it, if the Dwinns had an army then this never would've happened, this lot never would've got past the frontier. But"—Bert made sure to let that 'but' linger just as long as he could . . . in the vague hope of making it sound a little menacing, though he was silently convinced it sounded a little more like dementia—"unfortunately the gnomes *in charge of* the Domain don't believe that its gnomes really deserve to have any sort of a defence which means that any gnomes *at any time* can simply waltz on in here and take over."

This time the other gnome piped up. "We did all right 'ere," he said, "got rid of this lot jus' fine."

"Ah," Bert said, sticking his index finger up in the air . . . maybe because of some subconscious influence from Master Yorn, "but what about the next time, and the next, and the next, like I said up there to your leader, this certainly won't be the last time another Domain decides that they quite fancy a go at taking over the Dwinns."

The two gnomes exchanged glances. The rifle butt remained pointing at Bert's chest.

Bert decided that he really needed to push matters along just a little. "Look, who's telling you what to do here, that golden-bearded gnome, the one who's in charge?"

The two gnomes fixed Bert with blank gazes.

Bert felt Lax slip a little down his shoulder and he jostled him back into position. "You think that every time a Domain decides to cross the border you'll just run off and hide, allow them to trudge through your villages, through *your* homes, as you wait down here in these tunnels like a bunch of . . ." he waited for the perfect word to strike him then released ". . . *rats*."

"Hey!" the gnome with the rifle butt pointed at Bert's chest said, "We ain't no *rats*, buddy."

Bert sucked in a deep breath, decided to take his luck with that, admittedly offensive-looking rifle butt, and said, "Then why do you *act* like it then?"

This seemed to send the two gnomes into a spiralling confusion and Bert watched them, with no little delight, as they gave each other blank stare after blank stare.

Then the one who pointed the rifle butt at Bert's chest frowned at him, pouted just a touch and then said, "And this army, you're sayin' tha' if you get control, and tha', tha' you'll take us on?"

Bert decided that now wasn't a good time to be enigmatic so he settled for some vigorous nodding.

This seemed to swing the argument in his favour, and the two gnomes exchanged nods.

"All righ'," the one with the rifle butt pointed at Bert's chest said, "Whatcha wan' us to do?"

Bert pursed his lips and grabbed a hold of Lax, determined not to let him slip from his grasp and drop to the floor. "I want you to take me to your leader."

Another exchange of glances later and the gnomes gave him a pair of nods.

Bert looked at the rifle butt again, *still* pointed at his chest, and he said, "You know, that thing might work just a *touch* better if you turned it around the other way."

GETTING AWAY WITH IT

B ERT COULDN'T HELP but feel that tug at his gut—the rush of anticipation—as the pair of armed gnomes led him along the tunnel and, apparently, in the direction of their leader.

It also meant that he'd relieved the chamber of any guards at all, and so, if Ardull saw fit, he could spring his gnomes from that chamber where they were all supposed to be imprisoned.

What happened next would really depend on Ardull and what orders he saw fit to give his men.

Bert had given the two gnomes a crash course in holding the rifles: barrels away from you, fingers on the triggers . . . really Gunplay 101.

Now they were doing just fine.

Of the couple of gnomes they'd run into on their travels, up along the tunnels, the armed gnomes had seen them all off with a shake of the rifle here and there.

No one seemed to really oppose them heading upwards to go and see the leader.

Or hung around long enough, once they'd seen the gnomes had got the rifles the right way around, to ask just what Bert and Lax—those two *traitors*—were doing out of captivity.

In the end, they reached a smallish alcove in the underground lair, and the two gnomes glanced back at Bert and Lax, apparently asking for permission to carry onwards.

Bert made a gesture for the two of them to come to a halt, and for them to wait just where they were. Then, with Lax still leaning up against him, now past the drowsy stage and flat-out snoring, he staggered onwards to confront the leader: the golden-bearded gnome who sat at an improvised, shoddy wooden desk scrawling out something or other on parchment with a quill and wearing thin-framed, thick-lensed glasses to do so.

Bert waited a beat. Waited for the gnome to glance up from his paperwork. Registered his gawping look of surprise, then savoured his glancing about for a sign of guards. That momentary look of relief as he saw his two goons with their rifles—pointed the right way around—and then the shudder of realisation as he caught onto what was really going happening here.

Bert allowed himself a thin-lipped smile, though he took no joy from it.

Not *much* joy anyway.

The golden-bearded gnome glanced about himself as if he might suddenly come across some exit from this chamber. Perhaps he was thinking about getting stuck in with his teeth, doing his best to burrow his way out of this mess.

Maybe it was the rifle turned the right way around that

swung things for him because he laid his quill down beside the parchment on his desk and gave them a nervous smile. "Well, then," he said, "wha's it I can do for you?"

The two gnomes with the rifles bound the golden-bearded gnome's wrists and then shoved him off along the corridor.

Bert carried on after them, still doing his best to keep Lax upright in his hold, to stop him from fainting on him. Thinking about it, he might've been better off just leaving Lax down in the chamber with the rest of Ardull's men.

The benefit of hindsight, eh?

As they headed back down, Bert expected some sort of opposition to come from the rest of the gnomes about the place but they all gave the same look of defeat when they saw that their leader had been captured, his wrists bound.

That, Bert thought to himself, was the true Dwindian way.

These gnomes had just believed whatever it was that the golden-bearded gnome had told them, and, he supposed, on balance he'd done a decent job. After all, he'd got all these gnomes out of their villages and down underground to safety.

Now, though, it was time for the big boys to take over.

The ones that actually had a clue about what was going on.

And so, when one of the two gnomes escorting the golden-bearded gnome about turned to Bert and said, "So, we takin' orders from you nah, or wha'?" there was really nothing else for Bert to say except for "Yes."

A SWIFT REVERSAL

THINGS HAPPENED so quickly and without Ardull's knowledge that he couldn't help feeling just a touch suspicious. The way that Flaughterbert so simply managed to relieve those guards from the entrance of the chamber, to get them turned around and headed away. That had been Ardull and his men's opportunity to escape, and they hadn't wasted so much as a moment.

When they'd arrived back into the amphitheatre area, caught all those thousand or more gnomes sitting about on their backsides and looking completely stunned, he'd issued orders quickly to his men, to get them into prime, tactical positions.

Now that the guerrilla gnomes didn't have the element of surprise this was easily done.

One thing was for certain, these gnomes certainly weren't any match for a truly prepared and well-led band of professional soldiers.

Even if those soldiers were unarmed.

A couple of minutes later, Flaughterbert had returned still supporting his companion who'd got shot, and now with the golden-bearded gnome before them, his hands tied.

This had started off murmurs among the guerrilla gnomes but not so much as an angry guesture among them. It seemed that the very act of seeing their leader captured had the effect of nullifying any sort of anger or injustice they might've felt.

Ardull was quite glad about that.

The way that things turned out, from then on, Flaughterbert was swiftly appointed the new leader of the band of men, though Ardull made a point of sidling up beside him on the stage so that he might be seen before them too.

It would be extremely bad form, not to mention a dangerous precedent, to allow his gnomes to believe that he had surrendered control to Flaughterbert: a Dwindian.

There would be questions asked about *just who* was in charge here.

As Ardull looked over the files of his newly conscripted soldiers: women and children among them, he couldn't help but turn his mind to that perennial concern of his, the one that had bothered him no end for the past day and night.

The issue of his book of poetry.

And so, following Flaughterbert's jabbering at the rest of the amphitheatre, Ardull got hold of his translator and told him just what it was that he wished to impart to the crowd of guerrilla gnomes.

Ardull watched on as the words passed about the assembled guerrilla gnomes, how they chattered among themselves, the neighbours leaning into one another in a brief semblance of confusion. And then, miracle of miracles, one of the gnomes got to her feet and hoisted, above her head, his beloved spiral-ringed notebook, those familiar curled up, slightly yellowing pages that he'd spent so much time with in the course of this operation.

He felt every muscle in his body tightening as he observed the notebook's passage through the crowd, from one gnomic hand to the next, before finally reaching his translator who stood at the front row ready to receive it.

Ardull couldn't really believe what he'd just witnessed till he got the notebook in his hand, till he could grip it in his fist and see that first scrawled page of his poetical scribblings.

For the first time in what felt like an *awfully* long time, he was happy.

Inside and out.

He turned to take in Flaughterbert standing there, before the crowd, giving orders in Dwindish to them all, detailing out what was going to happen next, and Ardull realised that, really, he couldn't have cared less about what Flaughterbert was saying to them—in that moment he cared no longer about the success or failure of the operation realising what he'd really known all along.

That his soul was a poetical soul.

And that was *all* that mattered to him.

ONWARD FEARLESS SOLDIERS!

WHEN BERT emerged from the hole that served as the entrance to the guerrilla headquarters, the day was just dawning. It had been raining, as he could tell from the smell on the air, and the dampness of the grass as he steadied himself against the ground with the sturdy heel of his hand.

He chomped pensively on his fresh wad of fudge which he'd fished out from his knapsack.

The *last* wad of fudge he'd brought with him for the journey.

To be honest, he hadn't thought it would turn out to be such a grand palaver, what with him only having set out to meet with the Council, and to outline his propositions to them.

But it had ended up being really quite complicated.

More so than he'd anticipated.

He could hear the gentle murmur of his charges at his heels, all of them hauling themselves up and out of the hole in the ground, most of them armed with aforementioned rifles and rocks, and other such pieces of miscellanea that had ended up being used as makeshift weapons.

He stood by with just a touch of pride as he watched them all crawl out of the holes and assemble in a rag-tag row before him. He watched as Lax emerged from the hole, being helped out by a pair of Ardull's men.

He was glad to see that the colour—the *normal* colour—was beginning to return to his cheeks and that he was looking like he could support his own weight again . . . albeit still with the aid of those two gnomes of Ardull's.

Ardull himself emerged several moments later, flanked, as always, by his interpreter and that gnomic soldier, the one who'd captured them to start with, the one called Jeorge.

After a brief conversation, through the translator, Ardull agreed to sift through the charges and to weed out those who might be injured, or too weak for the battle ahead.

This turned out, as Bert noticed, to really be an operation in removing women and children from the ranks, though there was one, a veritable *battalion*, of square-shouldered women who must've been closing on two hundred years old, armed with rolling pins and pinny aprons who didn't seem likely to be shifted from the assembling army, no matter how much Ardull *attempted* to reason with them through his interpreter.

Lax, too, proved to be a very difficult case. He had snapped back to his normal state of mind, or so it seemed to Bert, and he was adamant that he wouldn't have his bloody-minded intention of going along for the ride stolen away from him.

That was fair enough, and Bert watched on as Lax attempted to push this point by taking several paces back and forth, limping heavily, holding up his arms as he did so to show that he really didn't need any help at all, that he would be just fine for battle.

This seemed to be enough to convince Ardull, and Lax was hurriedly armed with a sawn-off branch from a nearby tree . . . which, just like the dozens of these improvised weapons, was sharpened into quite a pointy point.

By the time that they'd gone through all these preparations, it was well into mid-morning and the sun was already doing a job of warming up the ground about them, sending that thick scent of soil wavering up into the air.

Bert looked over his troops for a last time, as if he might notice something with his inexpert eye that Ardull hadn't seen, and then, with a curt nod from Ardull, he issued the order for them to move forwards.

TAKING THE POWER BACK

B ERT SMELLED Cormersbarn before he'd so much as
caught a gimmer of it on the horizon. That stench of
horse, and gnome, manure was more distinctive even than the
angular rooftops, the multi-coloured tarps of the marketplaces,
or even the faecal-brown moat which surrounded the town.

The wall that he and Lax had previously scaled now didn't
seem like so much of an obstacle.

Why, the brickwork seemed, even from a long way off, to
present dinky footholds for an entire army such as the one he
now led to scale it.

As luck would have it, though, all the bridges were well and
truly in service today, and he caught the reflection of the sunrays
off the metal parts of creaking horse-drawn carts . . . the ones
that arrived from *other* Domains . . . as they made their way to
the afternoon markets.

Bert slicked his fudge over his tongue, manipulated it into a smooth paste, and then swallowed it down, knowing that there would be plenty of fudge later on, when he had successfully gone and conquered the place.

As they drew closer to the city walls, Bert felt his chest tighten just a touch, he wondered if the Council might've caught a clue about just what might be headed their way. That they might've instated some sort of a conscription service within the city following their meeting with Bert . . . but no, it was really nothing more than an afternoon stroll for Bert and his charges as they found a gap in the horse-drawn carts heading in over the bridge into the town, and then trudged on inside the city walls.

Getting into the main square proved equally as simple, with them facing no opposition whatsoever as they marched on over the cracked-up roads and brought the Seat of the Council into view ahead.

He looked over the blocky structure, the light-pink colour of the building, and breathed in that faint scent of cinnamon that seemed to cling to the place.

In many ways, he felt just like the first time he'd shown up here, a touch nervous, and ready to be sent packing like the country bumpkin he felt he really was.

But this time it was different.

This time he had brought an army with him.

The, unarmed, guards on the front steps off the palace exchanged glances and then, very swiftly, disappeared from sight.

Where they went Bert really couldn't say.

But he led his gnomes on forwards, through the hallways, and towards the Deliberation Room, the room where he'd been made to look a fool no more than a couple of days earlier.

In no time at all, Bert turned the doorknob and looked on in at the Council, all of them sitting there on their leather-uphol-stered chairs all of them arranged about the long, circular walnut desk.

All seven of the Council.

Bert couldn't quite recall their names, the only one that stood out for him was Chairwoman Maxine.

Her hair was nicely coifed today. Her lips painted that same crimson that Bert recalled from before. And her black eyes glowered at him as she sat with her wrists arched on the arms of her chair. Today she had on an emerald-green trouser suit with a lighter green blouse underneath. She arched an eyebrow as she took in Bert and his ragged army all crowding out the hallway behind him.

"This a *coup*, is it?" she said.

"You could call it that," Bert answered.

She arched her shoulders, breathing in deep, and then released an, apparently, long-held sigh all at once.

The other members of the Council, all sitting about her, stayed in their positions, all of them with somewhat frightened expressions set on their faces.

The only member of the Council that seemed totally unmoved by this situation was Chairwoman Maxine herself.

"So," she said, looking down at a piece of parchment on the table before her, "you decided that it'd be in your best interests to abet the enemy?"

Bert felt his gut tighten, but he told himself that what she was staying was simply standard, that these were the death throes of the soon-to-be-deposed despot.

He gave a stiff, humourless nod.

She leaned back in her chair, tilted her head back and looked at Bert from the bases of her eyes. "I don't think you *quite* comprehend what the Dwinns is about, do you?"

Bert blinked a couple of times. "I think, actually, I comprehend it just fine—these gnomes who've all come along with me today all comprehend this *just fine*."

She drew another deep breath but this time didn't breathe it out as a sigh, as Bert expected her to do. This time she glanced around her chair, to the cityscape all spread out behind her and all set in gilded afternoon sunlight.

He could tell that she was looking out over her empire for the very last time.

"The Dwinns," she said, almost murmuring it, saying it to herself, "this place, this place was always—*always*—supposed to be a refuge—a getaway from the rigours of Gnomelandia, that was how we wished to preserve it."

Bert felt himself flinch, and he was glad that she was turned away from him and so didn't notice.

Now she did turn back to face him, however, and continued. "My ancestors—the Council," she said, gesturing to the male and female gnomes, the Councilmen and women who surrounded her, "it has always been about preserving a certain *innocence* among the gnomes, *sheltering* them from the *cruel* outside world. That has always been our duty. To see off modern innovation, modern *technology* of Gnomelandia, and to bring up this Domain as a, well, I suppose you could call it an undisturbed garden."

Bert breathed in deep, tried to separate his emotions from this whole meeting.

That was the key.

On this whole conversation hung the future of the Dwinns— his children's future, his children's children's future.

"It might've worked better with an army," Bert said. "Where did all the tax money go if you never thought of investing it?"

She shrugged, pouted slightly. "How do you think we kept the Domain out of poverty? It was us who got money into circulation—kept the gnomes practising those little scams of theirs, doing the only thing they knew how. It was honest *primary* sector workers like yourself, like the farmers who kept everyone fed, that made the Dwinns work."

"Until now," Bert said, his throat dry, and his voice wavering just a touch.

"Until now," she agreed with a faint smile which slipped off her lips just as quickly. "Yes, I had hoped that we could put off *progress* for another decade, *another* time, but the way that the world works now"—she nodded to those soldiers in the hallway behind Bert—"the way that other Domains have set out their stall to expand and to take over *lesser* Domains, that surely means that the Dwinns will have to move with the times." She lifted the sleeve of her jacket up to inspect the button there . . . for what reason, Bert really didn't know. "And that means a wholesale clear-out, a new leaf, another form of government—the Dwinns being *annexed*, I suppose."

For the first time throughout this whole ordeal, throughout this whole *quest*, Bert found himself having certain doubts. Found himself feeling a little taut and unsure of himself. But he knew that he'd come so far down this road now and that there would be no turning back.

He reminded himself about how he'd felt, about how he was doing this for the future of Dwindians throughout the Domain, not just on some sort of a whim.

What the Council had been practising, *wilfully* keeping its gnomes in a sort of dependent slavery, why it sent shivers right down to his bones, and he was glad that he had seen fit to do away with the whole thing.

And so Bert turned around, met General Ardull's eye and gave him the nod.

Bert stood aside as the soldiers filed past him, approaching each member of the Council and taking them prisoner, tying their hands up with the same ropes that, only hours earlier, the guerrilla gnomes had used to take *them* prisoner.

They took Chairwoman Maxine prisoner last of all. She put up no fight. She even extended her captors the mercy of holding her hands behind her back for them to tie up.

As she was led past Bert she met his eye and then, with the corners of her mouth lifting slightly in a smile, said, "Good luck."

A NEW DAWN

T HREE MONTHS LATER, Bert stood up on the steps of the Seat of the Council, and looked down on the main square. He looked to the fully-armed security officers, about a dozen of them all told, all prowling about with rifles in their hands.

And all of them had their rifles turned the right way around.

Bert guessed that he'd been expecting just a little resistance from the Dwindians to the *coup de grace* that he'd just performed, the way that he'd abetted foreign powers in taking control of the Domain, but there had been no fight at all.

And he was only hearing good things from his gnomes on the ground all through the Domain, about how the new horse-drawn cart transport system was allowing gnomes everywhere to move between towns, to see things they'd never seen before and, as in several cases, to come and visit their capital Cormersbarn for the first time in their lives.

Yes, Bert could certainly say that he'd made a difference to his Domain, if nothing else.

And that was something he could be proud of.

Maybe all that letter writing of his hadn't been a waste of time after all.

Perhaps it'd been the perfect preparation for the task that awaited him now.

"Mr President?" came a voice beside him, the voice of Lax, now appointed as Special Presidential Assistant . . . a role which, like all the other roles that had come about in the new order of things, he had made up pretty much on the spot.

Bert eyed Lax, saw how he looked fully recovered now, though he still noticed how he limped about whenever he walked from room to room. Good thing that where administerial affairs were concerned there wasn't a great emphasis on tip-top physical shape.

Lax, there on a silver tray, bore a huge wedge of fudge which he was offering to Bert.

Bert took it from him with a smile and a word of thanks, then he turned to look out over the main square, and beyond to the slanted rooftops of Cormersbarn, his new home.

The *coup de grace* had entered its final stages, and so had the official proclamation that the Council would be stripped of all its previous powers and its members put out to pasture . . . which was another way of saying that they'd be installed in quaint little villages scattered about the Domain and allowed to live out their final days in peace.

One thing that Bert was certain about under his new regime was that he wouldn't permit any more acts of cruelty, whether it was with the swipe of a quill, or the shot of a rifle, between gnomes throughout his Domain.

His regime would be one of safety, and security, and organisation and education.

It was incredible really to think about the changes he'd wrought over the past few months alone, how he'd already overseen the implementation of the new school structure so that every gnome throughout the land would receive the same education—the same *rightful* education—before learning their place in this new world.

He had sold up his mountaintop mansion, and his independent mining operation with it, to a local cooperative in his home village of Earknork.

That, as he saw it, was the key now, that he needed to teach his gnomes—the Dwindian gnomes—how to fend for themselves so that they no longer had to rely on phony systems to keep them from starvation, he had to teach them that those scams they'd run their entire lives were just that: dishonest and no way for a self-respecting gnome to make a living.

He hoped, along with the influx of Juttilians to the Domain, that they would start making changes to the long-engrained Dwindian culture.

Changes for the better while all those bedrock questions of identity and belonging hung about, because there were certainly *good* aspects of Dwindians that bore preserving . . . though Bert was truly struggling to think of a specific example right now.

With Lax standing up alongside him, the two of them looking out over Cormersbarn, and the future, Bert couldn't help but feel intensely positive for the future.

He had won a diplomatic election, the gnomes of the

Dwinns had shown them that they really did want him, and that'd been a really nice massage for his ego, all things considered, after the unpleasantness of that vote among the guerrilla gnomes going against him.

Bert turned to Lax, saw that he was chomping on fudge himself, and then he said, draping his arm about his shoulder, "You know, I've got a feeling that everything's going to be *all right* from now on, how about you?"

Lax met his eye briefly and then cast his glance out over the cityscape too, apparently drinking it in for himself. Bert knew that Lax had been greatly enjoying his new role as Special Presidential Assistant, and particularly enjoyed throwing that title about town when he went out drinking in the evenings—Bert supposed that his luck with the lady gnomes had just about tripled when compared to his days as a blacksmith.

"Yeah," Lax said, "I'm feeling fine about this whole thing now."

Bert gave Lax a friendly pat on the shoulder, then brought his hands down to his belt buckle where he folded them up there, and looked on out with a satisfied sigh brewing at the base of his lungs. "And to think," he said, "that all this, one day, and if the gnomes permit it, might all be yours."

Lax startled at this remark, looked to Bert with bulging eyes. "You mean . . . ?"

Bert had only thought to raise this matter right now. This moment seemed the correct time. "Well," Bert continued, "it's not like I'm going to live forever, so I guess it's high time that I begin the process of grooming my successor, don't you think?"

Lax gaped a little at this news, and a fresh film of confusion settled in over his eyes. But he blinked it away, and then took on a steely grin. "Yes," he said, "that sounds like a great idea."

And so the two of them, chewing away merrily on their fudge, gazed on out over the rooftops of Cormersbarn with the steady knowledge that the future of the Dwinns would be assured for another generation to come, that the Dwinns would shuck its backward legacy and look, for the first time, to the future—embrace changing times.

There was work to be done before Bert could truly bring himself to settle down, for him to find that ever-elusive lady gnome and start up his own family.

But when he did decide that the time had come, he would feel safe in the knowledge that an appropriate successor would be standing by to take up the reins, never to allow the Dwinns to fall into such careless hands again.

And that, all things considered, was just about the best life's work he could think of.

A POEM FOR THE REVOLUTION

PLAIN-OLD Ardull Whithersnool could feel the heat of the bright-white stage lights even from the backstage area where he stood, leaning gently up against a wall of peeling light-cream paint. He could smell the mank of the wood floorboards of the stage from here, and it twisted his gut even despite the fudge he was chewing on vigorously, trying to rid himself of anything other than that overly sweet, sugary paste.

Out there, in the audience, he could hear mumbling as they waited for the compere to waddle out on stage to announce him. From where he stood, backstage, he could only see the faded red velvet curtain which formed the backdrop. And the lights all beaming down on it with their sallow glow.

It was only now that Ardull was convinced that this had been a mistake—a *big* mistake.

He clutched his notebook tighter, looked over his scribblings on it, the poem he'd composed during the course of the operation to seize control of the Dwinns even though he'd long ago memorised every line of it.

But he was certain that he couldn't remember it now.

And it would *surely* be impossible for him to stand up on that stage and actually *recite* it for all these gnomes.

No, no, no . . . just one *stupid* mistake that he'd allowed his wife to talk him into: how she'd seen that advertisement in the *Cormersbarn Gnomic News* asking for poets down here at the *Ceramics Café*.

But he'd felt that twinge in his gut, the one that'd forced him to follow his heart and to come down here.

Because how could he continue to go through with his poetry if he didn't have an audience?

He supposed that he'd have to come out of the closet eventually.

And his whole family was here too, all out there waiting in the audience: his wife, two sons, and daughter, all of them looking on with, no doubt, looks of great expectation.

And that wasn't the only thing he had to worry about.

No, he had had to translate his poems for his public, so that he would be able to get across his verse to the local gnomes here . . . and though he'd been taking lessons in Dwindish ever since he'd handed in his retirement to the army—studying all day in some cases—he really didn't feel any sort of confidence that his poetry would come across at all well.

He sucked in a deep breath, told himself that this was the time. That if he really intended to be a poet, if that was his dream, then now was the time for him to sink or swim, because why else would he have thrown in the towel on a lucrative career as a general?

He chomped on his fudge a little more and then took it down with a single swallow.

On stage, he heard a bell clanging, demanding that gnomes find their seats within the café, that the evening's recitals were about to commence.

This was it.

He could back out now if he wanted.

He could slink on out into the back alley.

Wait for his family on a curb somewhere, where they'd surely find him after they'd realised that he'd scarpered in fear . . . would they think any less of him if he couldn't do it?

Would they *disown* him as a coward if he couldn't give a clean performance?

This was their future too, after all, that he was playing with.

He really had to make a good shake of this.

But, before Ardull could get himself caught up in any more paranoiac thinking, he heard a hush go over the crowd, and the compere speak. Ardull listened to him, finding the Cormersbarn accent soothing—almost familiar now. He could quite easily hold a conversation with a Cormersbarn resident, though some of the out-of-town Dwindians were much harder for him to understand.

"Ladies and gentlemen," the compere said, all dressed up in a soggy-green waistcoat with a shiny purple-black bowtie sprouting from his collar. "Tonight our first reading shall be from Ardull Whithersnool."

The compere cleared his throat and the audience seemed just

impossibly quiet . . . Ardull wasn't sure what to take from that observation: would they bay for his blood?

The compere continued, "A Juttilian by birth, Ardull served in the army which liberated the Dwinns from its corrupt, contemptible rulers, and he comes here tonight with a special verse which he wrote partly while leading the operation."

There was a smattering of applause and then, ever so slowly, it built up, like a wave growing stronger and stronger as it gathered up the currents. And, soon enough, Ardull couldn't hear his own thoughts for the sound of clapping and he realised that he was blushing. That his palms were sweating as he clutched his notebook tight.

He breathed in deep, tried to get control of himself, as the compere finished up his prattle.

"Now, please give him a warm welcome, his first recital for us tonight, Ardull Whithersnool."

The clapping got louder still and Ardull flashed a glance to the compere who was now looking right at him, gesturing for him to step onto the stage.

Ardull held back another couple of moments. He braced himself, tried not to think about the audience which awaited him, and then he took a step forwards.

And then another.

Then another.

Before he knew it, he was standing before the audience, though they were lost in the bright spotlight which shone down on him. That made it easier. It was like he was alone, all up here, like he was just practising to himself in the bathroom mirror.

The applause reached a crescendo, gnomes rose to their feet

applauding him, and Ardull held up his hand simultaneously thanking them while wishing them to fall into a hush.

The clapping went on for another half a minute or so before it began to quieten.

And then, just like that, the room was deathly silent.

Only a cough here and there punctuating it.

Ardull stared off into the beam of light which shone on him and which hid his audience away. He still clutched his notebook in his fist but he knew, on gut instinct, that he didn't need it now, that he could deliver his poem for all these gnomes.

That they would give him a fair hearing.

He sucked in another breath, rocked his shoulders back, and then picked a spot in the glare from the spotlight to look—a way to focus his efforts.

Then he began.

"This," he said, "is entitled 'A Poem of Domination.'"

For some reason, when he said that last word, and in the Dwindian tongue, it seemed to echo about the hall before him, and to plumb the depths of the room. He was certain that he heard someone give a slight *gasp* at his pronunciation.

His teacher did tell him that his Dwindish was still greatly inflected by his sharp tongue and tendency to clip off vowel sounds.

"The green fields flow,
From out beneath,
They do bequeath,
The passing time,
And the battle to be fought."

As he sprouted the first verse he felt like his heart might burst from his chest . . . but, against all odds, it stayed put. He went on.

"The quiet hill, it waits,
And the wind blows, waiting also,
The trees, they stand on duty,
For the bloodless victory won,
And fought evermore."

He drew another breath, felt his shoulders being weighed down by some invisible pressure. But he kept going.

"A new dawn, a new hope,
Rivers flow refreshed,
Enemies sleep in their beds,
And a land, a land awaits,
It awaits to be conquered."

He listened for any reaction to his penultimate stanza. He had great hope for it, and everything he had ploughed into it would set up the final stanza perfectly.

All the power of the poem would be lost if the penultimate stanza did not do its job.

But every gnome in the room seemed to be holding their breath.

"When the new day it comes,
Others shall wish they were,
And others that they were not,

As the wishing well runs dry,
Our future lies still, holding its breath."

He stopped right there, and then looked up at the glare from the spotlight. Every nerve in his body seemed to be drawn tense and his mind felt like it might tear itself apart in his skull if he didn't take a profound breath right now.

But he just couldn't bring himself to break the perfect silence which dominated the hall.

Before the recital he'd instructed his wife and children not to break out into what he termed 'pity applause' after he'd finished.

He wanted to hear the true reaction to his work.

And then, just like that, as it dawned on the room that he had finished his poem, there was a *clap*, and then another. One after the next, he heard the gnomes breaking out into applause, just as they had before while celebrating his military achievements, only now it was for his art, and it felt about a million times better.

Soon the whole hall filled with the applause, and it became even more deafening than the applause they'd given him when he'd been announced in the first place.

All of a sudden, the spotlight dimmed a little, and someone turned the houselights up and he saw those smiling faces of the Dwindians, of those he'd come here to conquer, and who he'd ended up becoming one of.

And he could feel the warmth coming off them.

It filled him with pride.

Because now, now he'd found his place in the world, and it was Cormersbarn. This had *always* been the place for him. The place where he could bare his soul. Where he could have an audience for the art he'd cultivated his entire life. The life of bloodshed that he'd eschewed for one much better—much more noble.

And that gave him greater happiness than he could ever have imagined.

So he smiled.

AUTHOR'S NOTE

Thank you for taking the time to read one of my books. If you would like to hear about my latest releases you can sign up for my newsletter here: www.raymondsflex.com

Thanks for reading!

Raymond S Flex

Gnome Way Home
A Long Way Home Novel

Copyright © Raymond S Flex, 2014.
Published by DIB Books

Cover design and layout copyright © DIB Books, 2014.
Cover art copyright © Unholy Vault Designs / Shutterstock, 2014.